TROUBLE AT VALVERDE

Someone from Valverde freed the prisoners from a prison wagon and killed the guards. The next killing occurred at Soledad Ranch when the fugitives stole horses and fled southward. When Soledad riders went in pursuit they made a startling discovery; whoever it had been who had freed the men in the prison wagon was also planning to destroy the town of Valverde—and that is not all they learned; they could scarcely believe the rest of it!

TROUBLE AT VALVERDE

Buck Bradshaw

A Lythway Book

CHIVERS PRESS
BATH

First published in Great Britain 1987
by
Robert Hale Limited
This Large Print edition published by
Chivers Press
by arrangement with
Robert Hale Limited
1989

ISBN 0 7451 1015 0

British Library Cataloguing in Publication Data

Bradshaw, Buck
   Trouble at Valverde.
   I. Title
   823'.914 [F]
   ISBN 0–7451–1015–0

Printed and bound in Great Britain by
REDWOOD BURN LIMITED, Trowbridge, Wiltshire

CHAPTER ONE

VALVERDE COUNTRY

There was no springtime; winter with its biting cold and its startlingly clear dawns, its depthless silence and its empty horizons went out with a series of snow-flurry rainstorms that lasted three weeks and swelled the grasslands like saturated sponges. During that length of time there was neither blue sky nor sunshine, just an identical dreariness from day to day.

For stockmen it was a time of drudgery accompanied with caked mud, catch-up chores like mending harness, replacing leather grease-retainers on wagon axles and multiplying lice on cattle.

The final drizzle tapered off one night between bedtime and midnight, the sky miraculously cleared and by dawn a huge sun arose to pour pale gold brilliance in all directions and by ten o'clock it was hot. The land steamed and as old Jake Monroe the *remudero* said, if a man put his ear to the ground he would be able to hear new life stirring just below the surface.

He may have been correct because within five days the new grass made a pale mat as fine as hair and within ten more days of that hot

1

sunshine it was tall enough to make livestock feed and was darker in colour.

Jake knew about that too; all seasoned stockmen did: After winterlong survival on dead stalks and underbrush the animals fed greedily from dawn to dusk. But new grass was washy; it did not have any strength to it. Perhaps it was not supposed to; it was a tonic. It flushed out their systems and triggered slipping hair.

It also brought heavy cows to calving time and that was what brought the riders out. Calving cows sought seclusion for birthing. They would hide in arroyos and in brush-clumps, and they would be as still as stones while riders searched for them.

With old cows there was usually little to worry about in the actual birthing process; they'd been squeezing out their young for years and had no trouble. With first-calf heifers anything could happen, and occasionally did.

But that was not the basic worry of range cattlemen. It was the scent of blood and afterbirths which drew wolves and coyotes. Some old girls could jump up within minutes of delivering, ready to fight. With others exhaustion robbed them of the will and the strength to protect helpless calves.

Wolves would drag a baby calf a half-mile then tear it to pieces. Coyotes, smaller, less endowed for fighting a thousand-pound cow

2

with five-foot hooks, used stealth and numbers to do the same thing.

Some years the toll was worse than other years. About this anomaly Juan Mendez put the blame on late, wet springtimes. These, he said, drove hungry predators down from the mountains where they could find nothing to eat, and the afterbirth scent of a calving ground drew them like flies. He was also of the opinion that wolves at least, but perhaps not coyotes, were creatures whose intelligence told them when and where to go because their forefathers had been doing it for generations.

It was a tradition to them to return each calving season to the same places.

Bryan Alvarado had grown up in this country where most rangemen were of Spanish or Mexican descent, everyone was bilingual, and although in other places there was a noticeable separation between *gringos* and pepperbellies, in Bryan Alvarado's country there not only was almost no separation, there was an easy, good-natured acceptance of differences. It had been in existence so long the customs were hopelessly intermingled.

Too, there was a rather large population which was the result of a century of miscegenation. Bryan's mother had been blue-eyed, red-headed, with a peaches-and-cream Irish complexion. His father had been fair and handsome but with black hair and very

3

dark eyes. Bryan had been his mother's maiden name. Alvarado had been his father's name. In fact the Alvarado holdings were vast because four generations of Alvarados had been steadily adding to them.

Frank Miller the rangeboss often said that in seven years as foreman there still were miles of Rancho Soledad he had never ridden over.

But for the most part those were miles of upland timber country where the cattle did not go, and were not allowed to go, or they were the westward badlands, where alkali soil prevented grass from growing and the cattle never went very far into that country nor remained when they did go over there. Even the water was bad; it smelled of rotten eggs, tasted of sulphur, and was unpleasantly warm even in the dead of winter.

Also, Frank had been on the Soledad long enough to know where most of the cattle would be at any particular time of the riding season, as now, so when he sent Juan Mendez, Jim Fisk and Poker Flannery—whose real name was Earl Flannery—to the northwesterly calving country with Winchesters, he was not only banking on what he knew of cattle habits, but also upon something else—it had been a long wet winter, there had been no intervening springtime, and now with hot summer over the land, predators would be stalking the calving cows.

Frank was borrowing some of Juan Mendez's

4

half-wise, half-superstitious range lore but he did not believe that part about wolves being intelligent; he scoffed at that, saying the wolves were drawn by the scent, nothing more and nothing less.

The day was as clear as glass with a promise of heat later and Frank would have enjoyed riding with the others; three weeks of being yard-bound made everyone restless, but Bryan had told him the night before at the cookhouse he had something else in mind for his foreman so Frank stood out front of the massive old log barn watching Jim and Poker and Juan loping through the golden early morning with pure envy.

Frank Miller was a man of average height sinewy build, tough as rawhide with a quiet, thoughtful disposition. He had hired on at the ranch eleven years earlier, when he had been twenty, and he had been rangeboss for the last seven years, since the year Bryan's father had died. He was greying and blue-eyed and sun-bronzed.

He had a small private room off the back of the bunkhouse, which went with his position of authority. Opposite the bunkhouse was the large log cookhouse. Between it and the rambling old adobe main-house there were several utility buildings; a shoeing-shed, grainery, smokehouse with four-foot thick adobe walls, and upon the opposite side of the yard, between the bunkhouse and the log barn, there was a three-sided big log wagon shed, a storehouse which had loopholes in the walls and which had been the first structure built on Soledad ranch, a wash-house and corrals which went from the south side of the barn completely around behind the barn.

There were shade trees on both sides of the yard and up around the main-house, mostly cottonwoods (*alamos*) which shed white fluffy material like cotton each summer before their two-toned leaves came out.

Bryan lived alone in the main-house where there were six bedrooms, a huge kitchen and a large parlour. Not in Bryan's lifetime had the house ever been full but the earlier Alvarados had populated it very prolifically.

Bryan, at thirty-five should, according to all the customs of New Mexico, have had a robust wife and *niños* all over the place. This was a source of discussion among the mammas over at Valverde, the nearest town some ten miles southwest of the ranchyard, but at the ranch nothing was said about it and in fact because there were no other married men on the Soledad and therefore no women, no one even thought about it.

Bryan was a six-footer with grey eyes, a skin coloured copper by year-round exposure, and light brown hair. He had travelled but his world, in fact his whole life, was Soledad

6

Ranch. That was how he had been raised and that was how he had matured. To generations of Alvarados, Soledad had been a duchy.

When he went down across the empty yard to meet Frank in front of the barn his stride was purposeful. Unlike others in the Valverde country who had inherited, Bryan worked hard, managed well, and rarely slept in the middle of the day, which was the custom. Because of these things, and a few other departures from the traditional New Mexican stock-country way of life, other native New Mexicans grumbled about his *yanqui* ways. It was rumoured that he did not even make wine but drank whisky, nor did he go to church, except on very rare occasions, and he dipped his cattle, another *yanqui* innovation. For ten thousand years cattle had tolerated lice and scabies and whatnot. Dipped cattle did not smell pleasant, moreover it was necessary to dig a deep trench and fill it with water mixed with terrible-smelling disinfectant, and dunking range cattle was very hard and sometimes dangerous work.

This was what was on Bryan's mind now as he halted to lean on the barn tie-rack near Frank Miller. He had ordered tins of dip three weeks earlier. By now they should be at the corralyard in Valverde. If he and Frank drove over in a wagon this morning they could pick up the tins, get the supplies the *cocinero* needed, see if there was any mail, which there rarely

7

was, and get back to the yard by late evening.

Frank was willing. He explained about sending the riders after predators. Bryan nodded and looked down into the cool, gloomy barn, saw no shadowy movement down there and asked where the *remudero* was.

Frank gazed at his employer. 'Somewhere around. You can find him by following your nose.'

Bryan sighed. 'The liniment again?'

'Yeah. It was all that damp weather. Jake's joints are giving him hell.' Frank's tone of voice lifted a little. 'But the sun will help. It always does.'

Bryan considered the weathered, calm face of his rangeboss. 'I think he's got to be eighty, Frank. My father hired him when my father was a young man.'

This was something Frank Miller had come to accept long ago. It was about the last vestige of the old Southwestern-Spanish ranching tradition of keeping retainers until they died, then burying them on the ranch. Jake Monroe was an old Texan and had forgotten more about horses than either Frank or Bryan would ever know, even though he could no longer ride the green ones.

But his usefulness was very limited. Frank shrugged and his employer grinned at him. 'You're a pepperbelly at heart, Frank.'

The rangeboss showed perfect white teeth in

a broad smile. 'I guess so. Well; what else can people do with the old ones? Besides . . .' Frank hung fire before going on. 'Eleven years ago when he was still riding he was like a father to me.'

Bryan nodded his head. 'Yeah. Maybe it's something in the water.'

Frank laughed. 'Or the air . . . Or maybe when you eat tortillas most of your life and drink pulque you look different on the outside but you become a beaner on the inside.'

Bryan straightened up off the tie-rack. 'I'll get the cook's list.'

Frank went back down through the barn to find and bring in a team of driving horses. They were light animals; no one farmed so genuine harness horses weighing up to eighteen hundred pounds were a rarity. They used 'combination' horses, animals broke to saddle or harness and a big one weighed a thousand pounds, generally they were a hundred or so pounds lighter.

A great many things were different on the fringes of the South Desert. The law for example, was different. Northward up in Colorado, through Wyoming up to Montana where there had been nothing but Indian social orders for hundreds of years, the law like the social customs was still green, rude and lacking the generations of precedents that existed in New Mexico. Even the shared conviction of an eye for an eye was handled differently.

Hangropes were rare in New Mexico and lynch-ropes even rarer.

Someone had once said this was because there were so few suitable trees. That may have been true on the desert, but the Valverde country was north of the real desert. It had trees. It also had water and good soil and dark grass.

CHAPTER TWO

THE NEWS IN TOWN

Valverde was one of those places where timber and water, warmth and good feed had drawn animals for millennia. It was an old town; settlers digging water-wells had been turning up ancient pottery, tools, and skeletons for many years. At one time it had evidently been an area of extensive Indian farming. No one had any idea how long ago the area had been settled nor who the first settlers had been, except that they had been Indians.

Now, the massively thick mud walls had more blue-eyed storekeepers than brown-eyed ones but the place was still Spanish-Mexican in appearance, perhaps because it was easier to renovate than to build something from the ground up.

The roadway was wide and tree-shaded, the

atmosphere was not as languid as it had been a few generations earlier but it was still likely to become that way in the middle of the afternoon; the siesta-custom which the first *norteamericanos* scorned had lingered and now it was acceptable again, especially during the hottest time of the summer.

Bryan and Frank left their wagon in front of the general store and walked up to the stage company's office to see if the dip had arrived. It had, they were told by a harassed, wiry, small man who wore a green eye-shade instead of a hat. He took them out into the corralyard, which was an acre of palisaded dust, flies and parked vehicles, some propped up with wheels off, and showed them nine large tins along a shaded wall.

The stage company's Valverde superintendent scratched his head and eyed Bryan quizzically. 'That's one hell of a lot of medicine,' he said.

They left the yard heading for the saloon, another mud-walled, gloomy building without windows except in the front wall, and got two glasses of tepid beer. Mexican beer, called *cerveza*, with a higher alcoholic content than *yanqui* beer occasionally had bits of wood or cork in it, but it was wet and after covering ten miles under a hot sun what really mattered was that it was wet.

The barman was a burly Missourian named

Leland Potter. He was a friendly individual and probably knew more gossip than anyone else in Valverde. He combed his thinning hair down both sides of his head with a parting over the centre of his skull and he never smoked cigars but he was rarely without one in his mouth. He chewed them.

As he set up the two beers he said, 'You gents heard about the prison wagon?'

Bryan was raising his glass when he replied. 'No.'

Potter settled his paunch against his backbar looking pleased. Everyone in town knew about the prison wagon; finding someone who didn't know offered Leland a splendid opportunity to expound. 'They caught some Mex border-jumpers during a raid down near one of those little gourd-towns, tried 'em, sentenced 'em to prison and the wagon went down to get them. It come through Valverde three days ago on its way north to the prison at Mesa.'

Leland paused until his patrons had put down their empty glasses. 'Something happened. Folks found the wagon off the road. The driver an' guard was dead, the steel back-door was open an' the prisoners was gone along with the horses off the pole. Even took the boots off the dead men along with their guns and hats, shirts, even their britches.'

Leland waited for the reaction. Bryan asked how far north the wagon had got and Leland

12

smiled straight at him. 'Six, seven miles, right up where your seepage spring with the stone trough is. A posse went out from here and there's talk a federal deputy is on his way down from Mesa. The posse come back empty handed. The prisoners went almost due west leaving tracks all the way over your foothill country, then they cut up into the timber and the possemen lost 'em.'

Frank was rolling a smoke when he said, 'How many were there?'

'Six. Bad *hombres*. They darn near wiped out some little border town, women and all. It was a bad band. Most of 'em got back over the line but those six found some whisky and stayed behind to drink it—an' do a few other things.' Leland looked at the empty glasses. 'Re-fills?'

They paid up and went out into the rising heat to find the storekeeper and give him the supply list. He too mentioned the prison wagon episode, only he had something to add. 'One of those army patrols snuck up on them. They saw smoke rising above the town. If it had been anyone else they'd have shot them on the spot. Damned army never does anything right, does it?'

After the storekeeper walked away, frowning over the list Frank said, 'Every damned summer, eh?'

Bryan nodded. 'Someday they'll build a tall fence down there.'

Frank was sceptical. 'They'd burrow under it.'

'Maybe, but how would they get their horses under it? They don't do anything on foot. Nobody said what that town was called.'

It did not really matter. There were dozens of little gourd-towns down along the border with people living in them as poor as church-mice.

It did not take long for the storekeeper to fetch the supplies out to the wagon and, as they were pulling away in the direction of the corralyard Bryan said, 'I don't like it; with Jim and Poker and Juan up there near the foothills. Escaped prisoners need horses.'

Frank was silent as they pulled into the corralyard to load the tins. A large, burly Mexican yardman who had a badly pock-marked face and a big, warm smile came over to voluntarily help with the loading. He spoke in border Spanish and asked if they'd heard about the prison wagon. Frank grinned at him; that's all they'd heard since reaching town. The yardman nodded. It was all anyone had been talking about for the past three days, he said, and pitched the last heavy tin up to the tailgate for Bryan to arrange with the other tins. He leaned and mopped off sweat. 'The soldiers,' he said, 'will be after them.' Then he shrugged powerful shoulders.

Bryan dug for some silver but the yardman made a deprecating gesture and walked away.

They left Valverde by the north road, turned off it heading northwest and now the old wagon rode better. They always did with a load up near the back of the driver's seat. Putting the load over the rear axle made them ride worse.

Bryan studied the northerly foothills which had a faint blue haze over them. Frank said, 'We've got plenty of time, why don't you drive up there?'

Bryan angled the team and let the lines sag in his hands after the horses were moving in the new direction. They both studied the land. It appeared empty. There were many miles of it running east and west at the base of the low mountains. There were patches of underbrush, some rather extensive, which was what calvy cows looked for at birthing time.

Bryan looked worried and wagged his head. Frank was less upset. 'It'd be hard for six Mexicans to get down there without being seen, Bryan. I wouldn't want to try and sneak up on Jim or Juan or Poker with a gun in my hand.'

Bryan leaned back and shaded his eyes with his hatbrim. He was not by nature a worrier but today he had a sensation of uneasiness. 'They'll be desperate and they'll know possemen will be looking for them.' He straightened up a little. 'Dust. Look close to the hills and west a couple of miles.'

Frank squinted. It was indeed dust but if the riders were in pursuit of a wolf or perhaps a big cat they would be making dust.

The sun was high, there was no shade until the wagon got up to the nearest stand of brush, and that hazy blur made it nearly impossible to distinguish details.

But the tan plume of dust was moving along the base of the timbered slopes clearly discernible with the dark timber to background it.

They heard a gunshot, flattened by distance but unmistakable for what it was. They listened for other gunshots and there were none.

The dust stopped moving. Bryan whistled the horses over into a trot and Frank, who had been pouring tobacco into a troughed wheatstraw paper, lost half of it when they struck the first rock.

He tossed the paper away in disgust and re-set his hat. They skirted two acre-sized patches of flourishing underbrush and had a clear run in the direction of the diminishing dust. Frank took a chance and stood up to see better. There were horsemen up ahead but he could not count them so he sat down and said, 'It's less than six men.'

He was correct. By the time Bryan put the horses back into a steady walk it was possible to make out only three riders. They were turning back and evidently they had seen the wagon because they altered course to intercept it.

A very large buzzard circled far above in lazy

spirals, the only other moving creature as far as Frank could see. If there had been a dozen of the big birds circling in one place like that he would have watched them; it would have meant something, most likely a cow or calf, was dead up ahead somewhere.

Bryan fished beneath the seat, brought forth a canteen wrapped in burlap and offered Frank the first drink. They could make out the riders finally. It was Juan, Poker and Jim Fisk. Bryan drank deeply and used the back of his foot to shove the canteen back where the sun wouldn't strike it. He loosened a little. 'Well, they're safe and they got something.'

The riders saluted and the men with the wagon waved back. They met in a low grassy swale with the circling vulture watching.

Juan Mendez was smaller and slighter than his companions. He was also very dark. Jim Fisk was a large man, over six feet tall and correspondingly muscled-up. Poker Flannery had sorrel-coloured hair and skin that reddened in sunlight rather than tanned. He was taller than Juan but not as tall nor as thick as Jim. They dismounted to tell Bryan and the rangeboss they had stalked a large old dog-wolf, had got him out into the open then had ridden him down and killed him where he was crossing up out of open country toward the timber.

Juan smiled broadly and gestured with both hands as he reported that they had not found a single dead animal nor a wet cow without her calf. Juan made this announcement as though he were personally responsible for such good fortune and Frank laughed at him.

Bryan passed the canteen around while explaining about the prison wagon and the fugitive border-jumpers. Jim Fisk puckered his face. 'I told 'em I saw some fresh tracks,' he exclaimed. 'Two shod horses with big feet.' Jim thought, then said, 'Six fugitives and only two horses?'

No one had an answer to that, but Poker put forth a suggestion. 'Maybe four rode double and the other two ran along on foot. They could take turns riding.'

Bryan was more interested in the tracks than in how the fugitives had been travelling. 'Where did they go?' he asked Fisk and the large man looked helpless.

'I got no idea because we was after that old wolf. Most likely up into the trees; that's where I'd go if I was in their boots. We could track 'em and make sure, Bryan.'

'Let's head for the yard and maybe tomorrow we'll come up and look around,' Alvarado said, taking a little slack out the lines. He was relieved. He was also uncomfortable because Frank had never worried but he had known Bryan had been upset.

They turned southward with the sun changing from orange to rusty red. It was a long

18

trail back. They would be lucky if they reached the yard before full dark, and old Jinglebob the cook would not be pleased to have to make a late supper.

The riders wanted all the details of the escape. Bryan told them all he and Frank knew. Poker sucked his teeth for a while then speculated about rewards. 'Six of 'em might be worth a little money,' he said.

Frank scotched that. 'Let the army or the law handle it. We got to start gathering for the dipping.'

Poker looked pained but said nothing. Dipping cattle in hot weather meant getting dip on the hands and arms and sometimes splashed on the face. It burned and unless a man put plenty of lard over it, the skin peeled off. No one really liked dipping cattle. Even if a man managed not to get splashed he smelled of creosote for a week afterwards. Cattle did not seem to mind, once they got out of the trench and could rub on something.

They had wood-smoke scent in their faces when Poker returned to the subject of bounty money. 'There'd be at least maybe a hunnert dollars a head out for them.'

Frank had just completed rolling a smoke and said nothing until after he had lighted up. 'Poker, just let the bastards get out of the country, will you? We got a lot of work to do. Besides, six murderers as bad off as those fellers

19

are wouldn't be any picnic to try to find up in among the damned trees. If there's one thing Mexicans are good at it's laying ambushes.'

They entered the yard with two lights showing, one over at the bunkhouse, the other one at the cookshack. The wood-smoke smell was stronger as they got down in front of the barn to care for their mounts.

No one saw the *cocinero* come out and walk to the porch railing staring across at them, not even after he leaned far forward like a man being sick and placed his head atop both folded arms atop the railing.

They might have noticed but Juan had led his horse out back to be turned into the corral, and halted suddenly to look around, then call out, 'The gate's open. The horses are gone.'

Frank was the first one to reach Mendez. The others came up nearly as quickly and stood like statues. The gate was indeed hanging open. They usually kept at least ten horses corralled. There was not an animal in sight. Jim Fisk said, 'Poker, you was the last man to bring out a horse.'

Frank was walking toward the gate when he contradicted that. 'I was. I brought the team out an hour after you fellers left, and I latched it.'

From behind them over across the yard the cook raised a high wail. It stopped each of them in his tracks. Frank felt the cold sensation fill his stomach as he swung around.

CHAPTER THREE

JAKE

Instead of the customary two coal-oil lamps hanging from a cross-beam in the cookhouse there was only one, and its wick had not been trimmed lately nor had its mantle been cleaned, so the quality of light was poor, shadows lurked in all the corners, and as the men came in out of the night they missed seeing the pallet near the iron cook-stove until the *cocinero* turned from looking at the floor, his lined, leathery old face a dark mask of grief, then they went around the long table and halted.

In smoky light the blood looked black and there was a lot of it. Bryan sank to one knee and someone reached for an open bottle of whisky on the table to hand it over, but Bryan ignored that to lean down closer to the waxen old tired-looking face.

Jinglebob said, 'He's dead.'

He wasn't dead; Bryan could see faint movement of old Jake Monroe's bloody shirt-front. He raised the old man's head to shove a roll of the old blanketing under it then he said, 'Jake . . . ?'

21

There was no reply and the eyelids did not lift.

Bryan used a boot-knife to slice through the bloody shirt and expose the wound. It was a bullethole slightly below the heart on the right side. Someone breathed a shocked 'Jesus!' The cook leaned far over holding the whisky bottle toward Bryan Alvarado. 'He ain't dead? Here, get some of this down him.'

Bryan pushed the hand away. It was too late for a stimulant. In fact it was too late for anything. While gazing upon the tired, grey face Bryan said, 'How did it happen, Jinglebob?'

'I don't know, except that I was out back hangin' some laundry and there was a gunshot over by the barn so I run aroun' to the front porch. There was three other shots. I ducked inside for my Winchester then slipped out back an' down the far side of the cookhouse—and heard horses goin' in all directions.

'I snuck over there . . . The light was in my face but it looked like a small army of 'em all ridin' like the wind and Jake was lying . . .'

'Which direction?' big Jim Fisk asked gruffly.

'Southeast . . . They was out of range so I went over an' Jake was bleeding like a stuck hog. He looked at me like he was surprised as hell, started to speak then passed out. I carried him over here and made him comfortable on the

22

floor. The blood was runnin' out of him like a river . . . I tried to get him to talk but he ain't opened his eyes since I packed him over there.' The cook went to a sideboard and returned holding an old sixgun as grey as lead; if it had ever had bluing on it it was impossible to see any traces of it now.

Juan Mendez took the old gun used a thumbnail to loosen the cylinder-screw and dropped the cylinder into his hand. He held it to the poor light looking down the front of it, then he used a thin blade from his pocketknife to punch out a single empty casing and hold it out to be viewed.

Jake had got off one shot and that had probably been the first shot Jinglebob had heard.

Bryan sent the cook for a wet rag and mopped old Jake's face clean of corral dirt and flecks of blood. Possibly because the water was cold old Jake Monroe opened his eyes, looking directly at Bryan. Alvarado continued to gently wipe Jake's face as he smiled a little and said, 'Are you in much pain?'

Jake's lips did not part, his expression did not alter and although his eyes remained fixed upon the features of his employer they seemed to be drying. Frank Miller turned aside, the others stood like stones gazing at old Monroe whose breath came out in a bubbly sigh. Jake was dead.

Bryan continued washing Jake's face for a moment longer then leaned back and got heavily to his feet and tossed the rag aside. Juan handed him the spent casing and as Bryan turned it over in his fingers he said, 'Poker, take a lamp and see what you can make out in the dust out back of the barn.' As Flannery went to the door Bryan dropped the brass casing into a shirt pocket and raised his eyes to the cook. 'Six of them, Jinglebob?'

'Yeah, at least six of 'em. They was Messicans. I heard one of them yellin' somethin' to the others and someone answered him, then I couldn't hear no more.'

Jim was scowling. 'Southeast? We didn't see any sign of 'em cuttin' back away from the timber, Bryan.'

Juan shrugged. 'We didn't look hard, Jim.'

That was true, they had been more interested in riding down that marauding dog wolf than in horse-tracks.

Jinglebob had been following these exchanges with a frowning look of bafflement, so Bryan quietly told him about the renegades escaping from a prison wagon, and Jinglebob's face darkened. In his youth he had been a bad man to anger, and if most of the things which had sustained Jinglebob in his youth had departed years ago, his temper had neither departed nor mellowed.

But he said nothing, he simply stood looking

24

at the floor. He and old Jake Monroe were the oldest men on Soledad Ranch. They had been friends for many years. Now there was no one left to sit in the cookshack with Jinglebob drinking whiskied coffee, scorning modern rangemen and their ladylike ways.

It did not help either that Juan Mendez spoke across a long period of silence saying, 'It is God's will and he was very old with sore joints and a lot of pain. A man that old deserves his rest.'

Jinglebob fixed the slight Mexican with dark eyes set in muddy white. 'You damned beaner; you don't even let a man cool out before you decide he should have died anyway.'

Juan saw the fury opposite him and went to the table to sit down. He had nothing more to say.

They rolled old Jake in the soggy blankets and carried him over to the shoeing shed, wrapped him in burlap and canvas, put him where varmints wouldn't find him during the night and were filing out front when Jim Fisk joined them, still carrying a lamp.

'There's a pair of badly tuckered up horses out back near the trough. They been treated hard. I'll guess they came off the prison wagon. Out farther there's plenty of sign but a man can't make much out of it in the dark even with a lamp.'

Bryan asked if the tracks were toward the

southeast and Fisk nodded his head. 'Yes. As far out as I went, but sure as hell they won't keep in that direction. It'd take them right over to Valverde. We can pick it up in the morning, Bryan.'

Jinglebob's disposition had not softened. 'In the morning,' he snarled. 'In the mornin' them bastards can be two-thirds of the way back toward the border. They got good Soledad horses under 'em, for Chris'sake.'

Big Jim looked stonily at the older man. Jim did not take kindly to that tone of voice. 'You know anybody who can see in the dark?' he demanded.

Jinglebob did not relent nor wince under the large man's hostile stare. 'Y'don't have to see in the dark, damn it all. You know the direction . . . I wish I had a dollar for every time I've rode out like this. You're not goin' to ride up onto them but come daylight you'll be a hell of a lot closer to 'em than if you go wash and comb your hair and eat supper then go to bed like city-folks would do. Sleep when you should be riding, damn it all.'

Jim Fisk continued to regard the angry old man until Poker nudged him and turned aside to lead the way back out into the yard. When they halted Poker Flannery said, 'Our horses been rode a little today and there's not enough anyway, unless someone wants to ride the combination horses.'

Fisk glowered. 'In the damned dark?'

Poker did not raise his voice. 'He's right, Jim. Even if they cut south we'd be a hell of a lot closer to them come daylight.'

Juan Mendez was regarding his employer. In Spanish he said, 'Is it for us to go, then?'

Bryan looked past at stamping-mad old Jinglebob. 'Go wrap some meat and whatever you got in something. We'll pick it up on our way out of the barn,' then Alvarado went toward the barn and for a long moment Jinglebob gazed after them. He had heard what Fisk had said about the horses and although he wanted in the worst way to go along, he knew Bryan would turn him down if he asked. He went over to the cookshack.

They brought the horses up through the barn to the tie-rack out front and rigged them out. It was not something any of them liked doing; these animals had earned a rest but there was no alternative since the renegades had choused away the horses they had not ridden away on.

There was a little consolation in the fact that the horses'd had an hour or so to eat and roll and tank up at one of the stone troughs.

No one acted tired. They trooped to the bunkhouse for their booted carbines and an extra pocket-load of bullets and Jim Fisk had the presence of mind to dig out a fresh plug of Kentucky twist chewing tobacco and put it in a shirt pocket.

Old Jinglebob was waiting out front of his building with three bundles of food—and Jake's old sixgun which he handed to Poker Flannery. 'Use this when you pay 'em back,' he said.

Poker took the gun but when they were a mile out he shoved it into a saddle pocket. Those old guns would only kill a man if whoever was holding it was standing close enough to hear him breathing.

The horses seemed perky and willing but that fooled no one. They could not have recovered their stamina in an hour or an hour and a half. By the time the riders were on the outskirts of Valverde they would be beginning to lose their 'bottom'.

Jinglebob would have snorted like a bay steer if he'd been along; Bryan did indeed go southward for a fair distance but then he swung due eastward directly toward town. No one would expect those fleeing fugitives to approach Valverde.

But Bryan was not as interested in riding up onto the renegades as he was in getting fresh saddlestock under his men and himself and the closest place to do that was the liverybarn in town.

It was not actually very late when the Soledad crew appeared in darkness at the lower end of town, out in the back alley where they all piled off and followed their employer up through the feebly-lighted runway to the harness-room where a wispy old nightman with watery eyes, perpetual sniffles and a weak mouth blinked as though his heart was failing.

Bryan said they wanted fresh mounts, that their animals were tied out in the alley, and he wanted strong horses—*pronto*.

The old man sprang up and led the way down the runway. Whatever else he may have been the nightman knew saddle animals. Each one he led up was strong and fresh, not necessarily handsome nor even lacking the malevolent eye of trustworthy horses, but the kind of animal riders would want who expected to use them hard.

He did not say a word as he led up the horses and watched Alvarado and his riders start saddling them. Only when the horses were being led out front to be turned a couple of times before being mounted, did he finally speak. By then he had recovered from most of his fear.

'Mister Alvarado; my boss'll be wondering. He'll come aroun' about sunup.'

Bryan was toeing in to rise up as he answered. 'Tell him I'll pay him double his going rate and if any horse is injured he can come to the ranch and pick his own replacement.'

The nighthawk bobbed his head but without losing his worried expression as he watched the horsemen turn southward. The trouble with that kind of an offer, which was plumb fair for a fact, was that the liveryman might have a fit anyway.

A little later, after the nighthawk had ducked back to the harness-room to dig out his secreted bottle of whisky and re-fortify himself from it, after which he returned to the yard out front to again look southward, a soft, deep voice speaking from nearby darkness made him jump a foot.

He whirled and faced Constable Al Sutherland to whom he blurted out his side of what had just transpired and also his anxiety about having done as Mister Alvarado had told him to do.

Sutherland looked southward briefly then put a scowl upon the nightman. 'What did they say?'

'Nothing, Constable, just for me to bring up good horses . . . They was carrying Winchesters.'

Sutherland's scowl deepened. 'South?'

'Yes sir, south.'

Sutherland straightened up, ignored the hostler and looked down beyond the dark end of town for a long while.

CHAPTER FOUR

TOWARD DAWN

There was no point in riding hard until it was possible to see so Bryan set an easy gait. By the time the warm night was turning chilly, and after a lot of miles had been covered by men who'd had a long time to ponder, Juan Mendez asked his employer if that had been an old prison wagon or perhaps some kind of newfangled one.

Bryan said, 'Old; why?'

'Because every one of those things I've seen has been armoured all over.'

Bryan bobbed his head. 'That's the only kind I've ever seen too.'

'Well; they got heavy steel doors and are padlocked from the outside.'

For a few yards the men slouched along considering Mendez's implication. Finally, Frank Miller said, 'That's interestin' isn't it? The doors on those things got bars so close-set there's no way for a man on the inside to even get his fingers through, let alone his arm.'

Poker looked around. 'Someone opened the door from the outside?'

It was such an improbable idea that no one wanted to risk looking foolish by offering an affirmative answer but eventually Juan Mendez risked it. 'How else?'

No one spoke for an hour and by then, along with the cold, there was a thin pale band of light off in the east where it followed out the uneven contours of the horizon. Visability was still not good but it was better than it had been so they fanned out as they rode, looking for fresh horse-sign.

What they found was a horse. Frank came upon it in a shallow arroyo where it was picking grass with its bridle on. He whistled and waved his hat.

He had recognised the horse even before the others loped over to also get down and look for the brand. Frank removed the bridle but otherwise did not bother the horse. He said they could pick up the animal on their way back and pointed to the Soledad mark on the left shoulder. He also walked over to Bryan and opened his gloved hand to display something dark and sticky on the palm.

The other men crowded up. Frank said, 'It looks like maybe Jake didn't miss. It's blood.' He turned to look around. 'I think that if we look hard enough we're goin' to find a man who couldn't stay on a horse any longer.'

They re-mounted and with sixguns in their hands rode a zig-zagging grid until Juan Mendez acted upon a hunch and back-tracked the horse to a low jumble of rough-looking stones where two second-growth pines were growing. There, he found droppings to indicate that the loose horse had stood over here for a long time, perhaps for a couple of hours, before working his way westward in search of grass.

Juan stood in his stirrups to flag with his hat. He had no intention of raising his voice in a shout to attract the other men or of riding up into those boulders.

The men converged and Juan showed them what had attracted him to this place. Fisk and Flannery piled off dragging Winchesters with them. Bryan said he would ride around to the far side and approach from over there.

Visibility had been improving for more than an hour. It was possible to see as far as the twin pines and even among the big boulders where there were openings. Poker pointed to a path of disturbed earth where it seemed a man had been crawling.

Poker dropped his arm and said, 'Most likely dead; crawled in there like a snake and died.'

Fisk grinned. 'Go look,' he told his friend and got a sour glare.

They spread out. Over where Bryan was riding they could see him until he dismounted, then all they could see was the horse.

They were exposed. Whoever was among those rocks had not only good cover but the best kind of protection, huge old rocks twice as thick as a man.

Poker muttered a desire to have one of those cans charged with dynamite soldiers used for this kind of work, and knelt to lean on his Winchester and study the rocks.

There was not a sound. There weren't even any birds, and those pines were the only trees for a considerable distance.

Poker watched Fisk and Mendez inching forward and with a resigned growl began to also advance. All three of them were well within carbine range and would shortly also be within handgun range when Bryan stood up in among the rocks.

'He's here,' he called and turned to look downward as his riders stood straight up and started walking.

There was shade and fragrance from the two trees. There was also a kind of delayed night-gloom where the big rocks prevented pre-dawn light from reaching a small grassy place where a man was propped against a boulder, carbine across his lap and his head hanging forward onto his chest.

Fisk loomed up and said, 'Dead.'

It was probably the voice-sound which roused the sitting man but he was unable to raise the saddlegun before Juan Mendez put a foot on it and pushed it back down.

Mendez stared then said. 'He's not a Messican.'

They crowded up closer. Juan had been

34

correct. The grey, beard-stubbled face with its lustreless eyes and bloodless lips had an unkempt mop of nearly blond hair above it.

The men hunkered down and watched Bryan go over the man for an injury. He found it by getting blood on his fingers. The man had lost blood but the wound was not likely to prove fatal unless it got infected, which seemed probable because the man's clothing was stained and filthy.

A bullet had raked across the man's left hip ploughing a trough nearly as wide as a thumb and there was blood inside his boot and elsewhere. it was one of those wounds that even if the injured man'd had the time and the opportunity to staunch the gushing blood with a bandage, would be very hard to bandage properly.

Bryan took the carbine away from the man and tossed it aside. He did the same with the holstered Colt. The man's eyes moved but nothing else did.

Bryan leaned his own Winchester aside and said, 'Why didn't they help you?'

The man's gey-blue eyes went to Alvarado's face but he said nothing.

'Where are they going?' Alvarado asked and got the identical response—silence.

Juan Mendez stared from black eyes then got close, raised a trouser-leg to get at his boot-knife, and smiled broadly into the grey-blue eyes as they watched. 'He's not going to talk, so he won't be any good to us anyway.' Juan shrugged thin shoulders. 'But he's making us waste time.' Mendez leaned with the knife and no one moved to stop him.

The wounded man held back until the very last moment. He could feel the blade sideways against his throat and pulled his head back until it touched rock and said, 'South. Back down over the line. They'll make it. You're too far behind.'

Mendez was still poised to make a fast, sideways slash. From the expression on his dark face no one doubted but that he would do it.

Poker had a question. 'They was all supposed to be Mexicans.'

The grey-blue eyes moved tiredly toward Poker Flannery. 'They are. Six of 'em. Me, I was in the wagon with 'em. We was all tried and sentenced down on the border. Me, I was bein' held in the Sandrock jailhouse to be sent north when they brought in the six beaners. We was all put into the wagon together.'

'What were you tried for?' Fisk asked.

'Horse stealing.'

Bryan brought the conversation back where he wanted it. 'Which one of you shot an old man out behind a barn back up yonder where you stole the horses?'

The wounded fugitive gazed a long time at Alvarado before answering. 'I don't know. I never seen him but the others did. They was gabblin' like a bunch of chickens and someone fired. I didn't know there was anyone out there. I was bridling a horse when someone shot and hit me in the hip. I got astride and rode like hell. The Messicans fired off a few rounds then they came flaggin' it behind me . . . I couldn't keep up. I fell off and they laughed at me and kept on going. I crawled into these rocks . . . That's all. Except that that was yesterday in the late afternoon and they been ridin' all night, mister. You couldn't catch them if you had wings.'

Bryan felt for his makings and rolled a smoke as his men sat staring at the wounded horsethief. He was inclined to agree; they would not be able to overtake the renegades unless something happened far ahead to make the fleeing men slow their pace.

Frank came over and said, 'We're wastin' good time, Bryan. What do you want to do with this son of a bitch?'

They did the only thing they could do, they made a bandage of the outlaw's shirt and tied it tightly enough to stop the bleeding, which was down to a trickle by the time they had found him, and they gave him something to eat, a long drink from a canteen, then were leaving the rocks for their horses when he said, 'Wait a minute. How about one of you boys leadin' the horse back over here? I held onto the reins last night until I passed out and he got away.'

Juan Mendez grinned crookedly. He pointed and said, 'That's the owner of the horse.'

The outlaw looked upwards without showing embarrassment or remorse. 'Mister, I can maybe make it on horseback but I'll never make it crawling.'

Alvarado said nothing.

'All right,' the outlaw said. 'I'll trade you six Messicans for the horse . . . You hear me, mister?'

Alvarado nodded. 'I heard you. Keep on talking.'

'They're not goin' all the way south an' over the line. They saw the bank in that town up yonder. They talked about it all the way up the road. The reason I listened was because they never said that someday they'd like to come back and rob that bank, they said when they got out of the wagon they'd find horses and raid it. My Spanish's not real good but I know the difference when a man says he's maybe going to do something and when he's sure-as-hell going to do it.'

Bryan prompted the man when he paused. 'Keep talking.'

'Not unless you give me your word about the trade.'

There was a period of silence before Bryan nodded his head. 'You get the horse but that's all you get. Now talk!'

'They're going down to a place called Esparza. I know the town. It's about a mile north of the line. They got friends down there. They're goin' to round them up and come back up here and raid that bank and the town.'

Jim Fisk scoffed. 'You're lying. You said they was going over the border. Now to get us to help you you're concoctin' this story.'

The outlaw eyed big Jim for a moment with a hard look then spoke again. 'Pus-gut you put me on that horse an' take me back up to that town so's I can get some doctoring and they can put me in the jailhouse—and if I'm lyin' you can hang me for lettin' them get away by tellin' you this story. It's the gospel truth . . . An' why should I help you catch them except to get the horse so's I can get away? Folks like you don't mean a damned thing to me.'

Fisk was eyeing the wounded man with a deadly expression. 'Cut his damned throat, Juan. Lyin' or not he don't deserve to be alive.'

Bryan shook his head at Mendez then addressed the haggard-looking outlaw. 'Give us the right answer to one question and we'll take you back up to Valverde: How did they get the door open on the prison wagon?'

The outlaw looked balefully at Alvardo. 'A feller come out of that town and rode along behind the wagon for a ways, then loped up and flagged 'em to a halt. All I know beyond that is after he rode by the little window in the side of

39

the wagon he called out and the guards halted. They was talkin' when he shot 'em both right off the damned seat. Then he come back and unlocked the door with a key he took off one of the dead men.'

They stared. Frank Miller said, 'From town? What did he look like?'

The outlaw answered curtly. 'All I know was that he was wearin' a new beaver-belly hat and had ivory grips on his Colt. I never saw his face because the Mexicans was crowding up to climb out. By the time I got out too, he was already in the saddle heading back down the road in a lope.'

Not a word was spoken for a long time. Jim Fisk had lost his sceptical look but he was still regarding the outlaw. Juan sheathed his boot-knife and put a sharp stare upon Bryan. Juan clearly believed the wounded man. So did Poker Flannery but although he broke the long silence he did not say much.

'It's got to be true. Why would someone from town do that? It's got to be true though because those fellers inside the wagon sure as hell couldn't have shot the driver and guard even if they'd had guns.'

Bryan told Poker to go catch the loose horse, then he took the other men out of the rocks and shade to halt in early-day sunlight and say, 'I don't want to take the chance. If he's telling the truth we're the only ones who can warn

Constable Sutherland. If we ride down to Esparza after those bastards maybe we won't come back, but even if we do that's open desert down there; they could see us coming for five miles and ride down across the border so we'd lose them anyway.'

Juan Mendez agreed but for a different reason. 'If we go down there we'll be riding into that town cold; it's a gourd-town where they'd as soon kill a man for his hat and boots as look at him. If we stay up here we'll have a day, maybe two days, to lay a good ambush.'

Poker returned leading the saddleless horse. He had heard none of the discussion but as he tossed down the bridle and lead-shank he said, 'Bryan, it'd be better to let them come to us than for us to ride down there where they got friends and try to do anything. Damned well could work out so's none of us came back.'

They returned to the rocks for the wounded man and without any tenderness got him to his feet, carried him out of the rocks, put him down to re-tie the bandage, then hoisted him atop the horse.

He fainted and dropped like a stone.

Jim swore. They hoisted him astride again, this time on Jim's saddle with Fisk behind the cantle with one thick arm around the outlaw to support him, then they started slowly back up-country.

There was no noticeable heat until they had

41

rooftops in sight and, although there had been a lively discussion of the altered circumstances of their situation for a couple of hours, Jim Fisk had to support the outlaw all the way because even when he regained consciousness he never regained it for very long.

The liveryman was mounding the scourings from his barn stalls over across the back-alley out of an up-ended wheelbarrow when he saw them coming. He stood staring, even forgetting to bat at the flies which swarmed over him.

He recognised the saddlestock because he owned it but he was unable to recognise the riders until they were within a hundred or so yards of the lower end of Valverde, then he suddenly let go of the barrow and went loping up the back-alley in the direction of the jailhouse with not a whole lot of speed and no grace at all. Some folks were built for running on foot and some were not. The liveryman was not.

CHAPTER FIVE

COMPOUNDING TROUBLE

Al Sutherland returned with the liveryman. As soon as they entered the runway the liveryman faded away in the direction of his harness-room and Constable Sutherland stood gazing at the haggard, bloody man on the ground.

Bryan shot an annoyed glance in the direction of the harness-room, then faced Al Sutherland, who was the size of big Jim Fisk and maybe five to eight years older.

Bryan explained who the man was. He also related what the horsethief had told them and why they had gone south in their manhunt. The only thing he said which seemed to interest the constable was the part about the Mexican raiders returning to Valverde, and one other thing. He looked at Bryan with a scowl. 'We better get him up to the jailhouse and have Widow Billings look at the wound. He don't look to me like he's going to make it but before he cashes in I need more than just a fancy gun an' a new hat to identify the feller who unlocked that door.' He glanced around, then called in the direction of the harness-room for a blanket.

They put the wounded man atop it then all hands picked up the blanket and proceeded from the liverybarn up in the direction of the jailhouse. They were stared at but because it was still early in the morning there were not a lot of people abroad to watch the odd procession.

At the jailhouse they made the horsethief comfortable on a straw mattress atop a wall-bunk in one of the cells then returned to the office. As Constable Sutherland headed for the door Bryan Alvarado said he and his crew would be over at the cafe. Sutherland nodded and walked briskly away. He was sure the outlaw would die and wanted to talk to him before that happened. He needed precise information. The Soledad riders discussed this at the counter of the cafe. The general consensus was that Sutherland would not get much more than the outlaw had told them because the outlaw did not know much more.

The cafeman brought their platters of fried meat and potatoes, toast as soggy as a sweaty saddleblanket and coffee as bitter as original sin, then he went back to his kitchen with an expressionless face. They had entered the cafe before he'd had time to do much more than make coffee and fire up the cook-stove and although he was not normally an irascible man, being compelled to feed that many diners at one time before he really was ready did not do much to improve his disposition. But he knew those men, particularly Bryan Alvarado. It seemed wiser to say nothing.

Nevertheless he was consumed with curiosity. For one thing the Soledad riders had not shaved, for another they looked rumpled, as though none of them had been to bed for the last twenty-four hours, and finally, what really fascinated him was something Lee Potter had said when he'd come by for his morning coffee. Leland had seen those men and the town constable carrying what looked like a dead man up to the jailhouse in a blanket.

He shuffled back out front to re-fill coffee mugs and eyed Alvarado and his rangeboss. Neither one of them looked up from their food. The cafeman sighed and shuffled back to his cooking area.

Al Sutherland came in moments later, dropped down upon the counter and called out to the cafeman for coffee, then twisted toward Bryan to say, 'She wasn't real tickled to be routed out this early but she's over with him now. By the way, what's his name?'

Bryan chewed, swallowed, then said, 'I don't know.'

Sutherland was not greatly disappointed. 'I'll find out.'

Jim Fisk leaned to ask a question. 'What did Mrs Billings say about his chances?'

Sutherland accepted the coffee from the cafeman and blew on it before answering. 'I came over here before she'd finished lookin' him over.' He tasted the coffee. 'Bryan, do you believe him, or maybe he was blowin' smoke at you so's you'd help him?'

They had all been over this ground before. Bryan answered as cryptically as he had answered before while he was eating. 'I believe him.'

Sutherland put the cup down. 'One thing about it,' he said. 'Whether it happens or don't happen we're forewarned. If it don't happen all we'll be out is some time waiting, eh?'

Diners began trickling into the cafe, mostly single men from around town such as the blacksmith's helper, the clerk at the general store and the stage company's local representative, already with his green eyeshade in place.

Sutherland led the way across to his office and the moment he and Alvarado's riders were gone the cafe became a beehive of excited conversation with the proprietor taking a loud and active part.

Widow Billings was a short, burly woman with curly grey hair and bold eyes which looked direcly at people. She was the local midwife and over the years had also become as near as anyone ever had in Valverde to being the local healer. The Mexicans had several *curanderas* but they were not often consulted by *gringos* even though one or two were actually accomplished healers. It was their rituals that kept the *gringos* away, especially their custom of disembowelling a live chicken, splitting it wide and wrapping the warm carcass over open wounds to suck out any infection and poison.

Widow Billings employed no rituals and was blunt in her judgments, as now when she met the Soledad riders and the constable in his office and said, 'I have doused the wound with disinfectant powder. It stings and that brought

46

him around. He's not very talkative. He lay there staring at me, watching everything I did, and only when I had made a clean dressing and bandaged it did he open his mouth.'

Al Sutherland was interested. 'What did he say?'

The direct grey eyes met the lawman's gaze. 'He said—who the hell are you?'

Poker laughed and Widow Billings smiled. 'He's tough, Constable. He's lost a sight of blood but he's as tough as a boiled boot.'

Sutherland looked relieved. 'He won't die then?'

'If he's alive tomorrow morning I'd say he'll most likely make it,' the greying woman replied and let her gaze wander among the unshaven, rumpled men as she said, 'Who shot him?'

No one replied for a while, then Frank said, 'One of our men at Soledad. He was stealing horses with those Mexicans who escaped from the prison wagon.'

Widow Billings looked at Bryan. 'Was your rider hurt, Mister Alvarado?'

'He was killed, ma'am. That's why we went after them and found this one in some rocks.'

Widow Billings did not even blink when she said, 'Why did you bring him back alive?'

Al Sutherland cut into this discussion with a reproving comment. 'Because it's the law,' he said, and got a sulphurous look from the woman. But she said no more and walked to the

47

door before stating curtly that they had better feed their prisoner, prescribed whisky in his coffee, said she would return in the afternoon, and walked out into the brightening new day.

For a while after Widow Billings's departure the men stood in silence then Sutherland said he intended to talk to the prisoner, and remained in place which was his way of saying he meant to do this without an audience.

None of the Soledad riders particularly cared about the horsethief or what he might say, they were interested in the return of the *bandeleros*.

Bryan led them outside into the still chilly early morning brilliance and down to the liverybarn for their horses. On the way down there he said they might as well head for the ranch. At the earliest those brigands would not be able to return to the Valverde area until the following day, and very likely it being the Mexican custom to celebrate an escape with a day or two of carousing, they might not even come back for a week.

Juan Mendez was saddling up when the liveryman came hurrying down the runway from over across the road somewhere. Perhaps because Juan was the first man he encountered he said, 'Jesus! I just hear up at the cafe Valverde's goin' to be attacked by a Messican route army.'

All of them paused to gaze at the agitated liveryman. Mexican route armies ordinarily consisted of regiments of infantry, corps of cavalry and companies of artillery.

Six brigands had multiplied beyond what the Soledad men expected even though they were aware how exaggeration would be responsible for some embellishment. What interested Bryan, although he said nothing about it, was how Valverde's residents knew the brigands had mentioned coming back to raid the town.

It had not been exactly a secret, but it was interesting how fast the news had spread. He turned to lead his saddled horse out into the alley and left it to Frank Miller to reply to the badly upset liveryman, forgetting for the moment that Frank at times had a strange sense of humour. He heard Frank say, 'Yeah. An' there aren't enough U.S. soldiers down along the line to do more than look on. You better put your money in a coffee tin and bury it.'

They left town at a lope and Constable Sutherland arrived at the liverybarn while the proprietor was standing out back watching the riders grow small. Sutherland swore. The wounded prisoner up at his jailhouse had told him something he had wanted to pass on to Bryan Alvarado.

It was too late now.

There was an increasing warmth to the day by the time Bryan led his riders into the yard and to the tie-rack where they dismounted with Jinglebob watching from his cookhouse porch with a Winchester cradled in his arms. He came down to say he'd fire up the stove for breakfast. Frank told him they had eaten in town and Jinglebob looked relieved. They also told him about the wounded outlaw they had brought back to Valverde and what he had said about the impending raid. Jinglebob almost danced with anger. He wanted to be over there when those Mexicans arrived.

The men scrubbed, shaved, fed the livestock and pulled out a light wagon with which to carry Jake Monroe out to the old ranch graveyard.

It used up most of what remained of the day to get the hole dug among the other graves out there, and hold their private ranch services, and afterwards no one was very talkative. Jake had not been avenged but there was a possibility that he still might be.

Poker returned Monroe's old grey sixshooter to Jinglebob. His blankets, saddlery and warbag were packed away in the storeroom and while just about every vestige of his presence had been removed from the bunkhouse, in some ways the emptiness of his corner bunk, stripped down to the rope springs, was worse than seeing his effects over there.

By suppertime the men were hungry. Jinglebob's carbine was conspicuously notable leaning beside the front door of the cookshack and for the first time anyone could remember the *cocinero* was wearing a shell-belt and holstered Colt.

The riders exchanged glances but nothing was said.

What they discussed, with Jinglebob listening from over by the stove, was that rider from Valverde who had shot the driver and guard off the seat of the prison wagon and had then freed the prisoners.

The baffling part of this was less who he had been than why he had done it. Juan Mendez was of the opinion that it had not been planned; if it had been, he said, why wouldn't the rider from town have waited at least until the wagon was farther along, up the pass among the trees for example, where he would have run no risk of being seen?

Frank Miller nodded about that. 'Why free them in open country? They were just lucky to have got as far as they did before someone saw them.'

Poker listened and ate, washed it down with coffee and when there was a lull put forth his ideas. 'It was a Messican. They always stick together. Some beaner in town resented seein' those other Mexicans bein' taken up to Mesa to prison.' Poker paused to drain his coffee cup before continuing. 'Sutherland ought to bring in a jailhouse full of 'em an' twist a few arms. Hell, that was in broad daylight. Don't tell me someone in town didn't see a feller ride north after the wagon—if he'd rode north from Mex-town over behind Main Street, *they'd* have seen him an' they wouldn't tell anyone. That's how they are. Thicker'n hair on a dog's back.'

Poker arose to refill his cup at the stove. From over there he added a little more, and this time held the attention of every man in the big old room.

'I know Messicans and I'll tell you somethin' else. Frank wasn't too far off when he scairt the pee out of the liveryman in town. It won't be no route army from south of the border, but there'll be local Messicans who'll jump at the chance to go on a raidin' spree when those other sons of bitches come back up here. It won't be just those six raiders, believe me.'

Poker returned, sat down, tasted the coffee and settled back to roll a smoke to go with it.

'It wouldn't be just those six anyway,' Jim Fisk muttered. 'I'd like to know how many friends they'll have along from down at that gourd-town.'

Juan pushed away an empty plate and leaned back looking at Poker Flannery. Poker saw the look, reddened, then as he reached for his coffee cup he said, 'Juan, no offence. You know what I mean anyway.'

Mendez did not say whether he knew or not, he arose and walked out of the cookhouse leaving an awkward silence in his wake.

Jinglebob grumbled from over by the stove.

52

'That's the trouble in this country. When a man says "Messican" he means it in a hunnert different ways.'

Jinglebob did not elaborate, the awkwardness remained, Bryan finally finished and arose to go outside. The other men trooped after him. There was no sign of Juan at the bunkhouse so Bryan left the others and strolled around to the corrals.

Mendez was leaning back there watching the horses eat and did not turn as his employer came up, also leaned, and rested a booted foot on the bottom corral stringer.

In Spanish he said, 'You are not that sensitive, Juan.'

Mendez shrugged thin shoulders and replied in English. 'I shouldn't be, should I? I've heard it all my life. Sometimes, though, it sticks in my craw.'

Alvarado understood. He had never encountered it himself but he had known many men who had encountered it. He said, 'Poker'd tear the head off of anyone who picked on you. So would Jim and old Jinglebob. Juan, if they thought of you as a Mexican they'd never say things like that in front of you. Poker was talking about Mexicans from below the border.' Bryan slapped Mendez on the shoulder and grinned at him. 'Do you know what they would call you down there?'

Mendez turned, beginning to smile a little.

'*Gringo*.'

'That's right. You'd be a *gringo* to natives of Mexico.'

Mendez's smile stopped short of broadening. 'That's like being caught between a rock and a hard place isn't it?'

Alvarado removed his foot from the stringer ready to walk away. 'No, because you don't belong down there. This is your place and these are your friends. They prove it when they say things in front of you they wouldn't say in front of those men from below the line. They trust you, they confide in you because you are one of us. Come on, let's go over and sit in on the poker game.'

Mendez stepped back to accompany Alvarado. As they walked away from the corrals he said, 'If Poker's right, if the Mexicans over in Valverde join those border-jumpers when they get up here to raid the town . . .' He did not finish it, he suddenly stopped and looked at Bryan Alvarado. 'That rider who freed the prisoners—suppose Poker was right and he was a Valverde Mexican . . . If there's a fight sure as hell some of the local people are going to kill Mexicans, Bryan.'

Alvarado had not considered any of this so he stood in silence until his rider spoke again.

'I'm goin' to find out if he really was a Mexican. You go ahead and sit in on the poker game. I'm going to saddle up and ride over to

Mex-town.'

CHAPTER SIX

A FRESH RIDDLE

Al Sutherland arrived in the darkness about the time the bunkhouse poker-session was breaking up and the men were preparing to bed down.

Bryan left the bunkhouse and saw Sutherland tying his horse. He stood in motionless surprise for a moment then strolled down there as the constable was loosening the cincha. Sutherland glanced over his shoulder then said, 'Something that horsethief didn't tell you, Bryan. Those border-jumpers looted the hell out of a couple of towns before they dusted it south of the line and those six that got caught had another reason for being down there.'

Sutherland turned with his back to the horse. 'The horsethief listened to them talking about that. A *gringo* bought the gold they looted. They was supposed to wait for him in Esparza. They did, but they got to drinking. They was to get the money for the gold then dust it over the line and meet their partners in some town down there.'

Bryan stared at the lawman. 'Did whoever-he-was arrive in Esparza?'

'Yeah. They handed over the gold and he handed over the money. Then they kept drinking instead of high-tailin' over the line.'

Bryan stepped closer to lean on the tie-rack. 'He didn't say anything about that to us, Al.'

'He was a sick man, Bryan. He thought he was going to die. He wanted to get somewhere so's he could get taken care of. When I asked him if he'd told you any of this he said if you'd of asked he would have because he didn't care what happened to the Mexicans. They weren't friends of his. He never saw any of them before he was pushed into the prison wagon with them.'

Bryan was puzzled. 'Did they say it was the same man who freed them and shot the guards on the prison wagon?'

'They didn't tell him that but after they got up into the timber and could look southward from up there and saw your buildings, they said they'd go down and raid you for horses, and if they got caught they'd get a message to their *gringo* friend to help them escape again.' Sutherland was looking steadily at Alvarado. 'As far as I'm concerned that means the son of a bitch lives in Valverde.'

Bryan started to roll a smoke. As he was doing this he told Constable Sutherland what Juan Mendez had said and where he had gone. He lighted up, trickled smoke and met the lawman's sober gaze. 'If my riders weren't worn

56

out I'd take them over there, Al. I don't want anything to happen to Juan.'

Sutherland lifted his hat, scratched vigorously and re-set the hat, then he blew out a big breath and also settled against the tie-rack. 'He knows a lot of the people in Mex-town, Bryan. He'd be a lot safer than I'd be going down there at night askin' around.'

Bryan did not believe that. 'I don't think so, Al, because after he's been nosing around sure as hell someone is going to go find that *gringo* and warn him that Juan Mendez is trying to find out who he is.'

'You let him go, Bryan.'

That was true. 'Yeah. Until you rode out here and told me all that other stuff I didn't really believe Juan'd be in much danger. Nothing he couldn't handle anyway. Now I think different. Juan's lookin' for a Mexican, not a *gringo* . . . I think I'd better ride back with you. Juan could walk right down someone's gunbarrel without any idea who his man is, or he could get a knife in the back.'

Sutherland shrugged, then settled thoughtfully upon the rack while Alvarado went down through the barn for a saddlehorse. When he led the animal out of the barn to be mounted he said, 'A new beaver-belly hat and a gun with ivory handles. That don't sound like a Mexican does it?'

They rode out of the yard side by side. Only

57

one man saw them go. Jinglebob was dozing on the back porch with some laced coffee, his boots off, his feet upon the porch railing and heard them go past. He became wide awake. He thought one of them was the constable from town but was not sure, but he would have known his employer on an even darker night. Every man had his own way of sitting a saddle.

Jinglebob wiggled his toes, watched them out of sight, then drained his cup and padded back inside. He was tired, a little smoked up from the whisky, and had no reason to be worried so he went into his little lean-to room off the cookshack and bedded down.

It was a pleasant night, there was not a cloud in the sky so every star up there was reflecting light earthward, and although there was a moon it was only a week or so old so it contributed very little to the eerie soft brightness.

Constable Sutherland was deep in thought as to the identity of that individual with the new hat and ivory-handled sixgun. He knew everyone in Valverde, even most of the people over behind Main Street in Mex-town. The only person he could think of who owned a handgun with ivory grips was the saloonman, Leland Potter, and he never wore it. It was kept hanging on a peg in the backbar wall. He had taken it away from a drunk cowboy years back and had said every time someone admired the gun he had it hanging there so that if the cowboy ever came through again Potter could return it to him.

But all that meant was that Potter's gun was in plain sight. There could be a dozen other guns around town with ivory handles, lying in drawers or kept under pillows for household protection. And ivory grips were not that unusual, when it came right down to it, but to his knowledge no one carried such a fancy gun.

Sutherland was still wrestling with this when Bryan turned and said, 'Did the horsethief tell you his name?'

He had, but Sutherland's expression was sceptical when he repeated it. 'Charley Bright . . . I got a dodger on a Charley Bright. I think the horsethief maybe knew him some time, but Charley Bright was killed in west Texas three years ago trying to run off someone's loose-stock. It was in the newspapers.' Sutherland reached to button his jacket because the night was cooling down. 'I'll send down there in a day or two. The description on my Charley Bright dodger only says he was about thirty-five years old and about six feet tall. That could fit just about anyone.'

For a while as they rode along the constable was quiet, but when they had town-lights in sight he straightened a little in the saddle and said, 'Come morning I got to call a meeting in the fire house and tell folks what we know. Then I got to send out some scouts to keep watch a few miles below town. I hate to hold that meeting; it's going to scare the whey out of everyone and if those raiders don't show up I'm goin' to look like the biggest damned fool this side of Denver.'

Bryan said, 'You don't doubt him do you?'

'No, I believe he told the truth. What I'm a lot less sure of, Bryan, is that those Messicans won't decide to go back south of the border and forget about us. At least for a while. You know how they are; one day they're all excited about something and the next day they've forgot about that and got some other wild notion.'

Bryan concentrated on the infrequent lights up ahead. He too remembered that fancy-handled sixgun in Leland Potter's saloon. As they were heading toward the west-side back alley he said, 'Do you know an old Mexican named Tiburcio Velasquez?'

Sutherland nodded. 'What about him?'

'He rode for my father.'

'And you're goin' to roust him out of bed tonight?'

'Yeah. To start with. But first I'm going among the *cantinas*. Juan could be in one of them. It's pretty late, though. He might have bedded down, and that could make it harder to find him.'

Sutherland lightly scratched the tip of his nose. What he was thinking required tact to put into words so they got to the rear of the

60

liverybarn before he finally spoke again. 'Y'know, Bryan, Juan's a young feller.'

They were dismounting when Alvarado stared quizzically at his companion. Before he could respond Constable Sutherland said, 'I better go along with you.'

The nighthawk came shuffling out back, attracted by their voices. The moment he saw who was back there he had an attack of the sniffles and made a reasonable attempt to mitigate this condition by lustily blowing his nose.

Even from across the saddle from the hostler Bryan smelled the whisky on his breath, or something anyway; it put him in mind of ether.

As the nighthawk was taking their reins to lead the animals up the runway to be cared for Bryan asked him if he had handled another Soledad ranch horse tonight and the old man bobbed his head. 'Yes. Nice sorrel with your mark on his left shoulder. I'll show him to you.'

'Did you recognise the rider?' Bryan asked, following his horse inside.

'Well, he's a Messican an' he rides for you. That's all I know about him. I've seen him with you and your other men around town. Thin feller, not too tall, wiry as a piece of old rawhide, carryin' an ivory-handled sixgun.'

Bryan and the constable stopped in their tracks. The nighthawk continued forward to a rack in front of the harness-room before

61

removing the saddles.

Al Sutherland walked up there and said, 'Are you sure about the gun?'

The hostler turned, saw the steady way they were looking at him and had another sneezing attack. When it was over he bobbed his head up and down like an apple on a string. 'Yes sir, I'm sure because I saw it on him when he dismounted and handed me the reins. Ivory-handled sixgun.'

Sutherland led the way up out of the barn to the open area beyond, where several big old cottonwood trees were shedding. There were only three or four lighted windows the full length of the roadway. Sutherland stopped and turned. 'Did that sound right to you, Bryan?'

Alvarado had never seen Juan Mendez with such a sidearm. That did not mean he didn't own such a weapon but as long as he had ridden for Soledad he had never worn such a weapon, at least not to Alvarado's knowledge.

It did not sound right to him. 'Juan's gun is old with most of the bluing worn off and it's got the same hard-rubber handles it came with.'

Sutherland raised his head and scratched again, re-set the hat and turned to peer down into the barn where the old man was shuffling around their horses. He strode back down there with Alvarado at his heels. The nighthawk looked at them with a watery-eyed smile. 'Forget somethin' gents?'

Sutherland said, 'Are you sure that was the same man you've seen around town with the Soledad riders?'

The old man began to look frightened. 'Well, he was ridin' a Soledad horse and he sure looked like that feller. Skinny feller, not too big. 'Course it's dark tonight an' my eyes ain't all they once was.' The nighthawk was beginning to quake. 'Constable, I just naturally figured it was the Messican who rides for Soledad, but I could be wrong y'know. I don't want to get no one into trouble.'

Bryan was watching the hostler. He was convinced that the man had seen Juan Mendez. He caught Sutherland's eye and jerked his head. When they were back out near the cottonwood trees again he said, 'Let's go make a round of Mex-town. If it was Juan and he's wearing a gun with ivory grips he'll have an explanation.'

Sutherland looked askance at his companion. Bryan saw this and wagged his head. 'Al, I can't explain the fancy gun but I can tell you this for a fact: Juan was with me and the rest of my crew heading home from the north range when those raiders hit the ranch, killed Jake and stole those horses.'

Sutherland strolled thoughtfully beside Alvarado, head down, when he said, 'I wasn't thinkin' of that, Bryan. I was thinkin' of the man who shot the guards and freed those prisoners.'

Bryan shook his head vehemently. 'It couldn't have been Juan.'

'Were you with him when that happened, did you have him in sight?'

'No. Frank and I were returning from town in the wagon ... Al, let's go talk to your prisoner.'

'He said he didn't see the man who freed them.'

'Yeah, I know, but he also said he caught a glimpse of him as he rode past the barred window in the wagon, and again while the Mexicans were piling out of the wagon. All I want from him is a general description: Was that man six feet tall or five feet tall; was he skinny and wiry or was he maybe average and not skinny.'

CHAPTER SEVEN

A GUN

The prisoner had been scrubbed and shaved. Someone had found old but clean clothing for him. When he awakened and looked up his eyes were no longer bloodshot and dull.

Constable Sutherland wasted no time. He asked for a description of the man who had

64

ridden up from Valverde to free the occupants of the prison wagon, and the outlaw gave a predictable reply.

'I already told you I didn't see him; only when he rode past the barred window and again when the Messicans was crowding up to jump down, and all I saw then was his back. He was headin' south in a lope. Fancy new silver-belly coloured hat an' a sixgun with ivory grips.'

Sutherland said, 'Mexican or *gringo*?'

The horsethief sat up and propped his head on one hand. He frowned then said, '*Gringo*.'

'Tall or short, skinny or fat?'

Again the horsethief frowned at the floor for a moment. 'Thinkin' back,' he muttered, and raised his eyes to the lawman, 'He wasn't skinny. He was maybe about average height . . . Sort of husky from the back. But that's just an impression I got. The gun I remember and the new grey hat. The rest of it . . . Yeah, he was sort of husky.'

'Not short?' asked Alvarado, and the prisoner swung his gaze a little. 'No, he wasn't short, but he wasn't tall either. About average height.' The prisoner looked back at Al Sutherland. 'If you got someone in mind don't expect me to identify him. I didn't get a good look at him, and I was too busy gettin' out to pay much attention to him anyway.'

Constable Sutherland relaxed a little, considered his prisoner with the anxiety gone

65

out of his face, and said, 'Kind of strange what a man can recollect when he don't think he can isn't it?' Then in the same detached tone of voice he said, 'You're not Charley Bright. He was killed three years ago in west Texas running off someone's livestock.'

The prisoner gazed sceptically at the big lawman, then showed a ghost of a tough smile down around his lips. 'Constable, you don't always want to believe what you read in newspapers or what someone tells you . . . I got a scar on my back. Ask the lady who washed me. They left me for dead and went after their horses and drove 'em back in a dead run. I come to in the middle of the night half froze, and it took me until noon of the next day to reach a Mex goat ranch. They put me to bed. I was six weeks getting well enough to ride again.'

Bryan leaned on the barred front wall of the cell regarding the wounded horsethief. He looked different now; he was clean and shaved and seemed not to be in much pain. He looked Sutherland in the eye when he spoke and he did not sound like a man who lied.

The constable must have had about the same impression because after re-locking the door and leading the way to his office he said, 'All right, he's Charley Bright. Can you tell me why he'd use his own name when there's a dodger out on him?'

Alvarado ignored the question. 'The man with the new hat didn't sound much like my rider, did he?'

Sutherland sighed as he turned toward the door. 'Let's go find Mendez . . . No he didn't sound like him an' I never said it was Mendez.'

Bryan grinned sardonically at the big man's back and folowed him out into the chilly late night.

There were two ways to reach Mex-town, which was east of Main Street over behind the business establishments. One way was to use the upper and lower roadways which had paths leading behind town. The second way was to go down through any of the narrow little spaces between some of the buildings which were called dog-trots and which invariably smelled because they were convenient places for beer-drinkers to get relief.

Sutherland led off down the narrow place between Lee Potter's saloon and the harness works which was south of the saloon. Beyond, there was almost total darkness. Most Mexicans were very poor but even the ones who could afford coal oil and lamps instead of the customary candles did not burn lights very long after sundown.

There was an occasional light and as the two dark shadows passed one adobe residence they heard a woman singing softly to a whimpering infant by feeble candlelight.

Sutherland paused in the dust to jut his chin in the direction of a lighted building upon the opposite side of the broad plaza. 'Garcia's saloon.' Alvarado nodded. He knew the place. 'I'm glad he's still up; if anyone knows what happens over here it's old Garcia.'

But when they crossed the plaza Garcia's door was barred from the inside. Sutherland said something in annoyance and struck the door with a big gloved fist. He had to strike it three times before they heard someone lifting down the *tranca*, then a mop of awry grey hair above a very dark and deeply lined face peered belligerently out and rattled off something in angry Spanish.

Al Sutherland ignored the imprecations, pushed the man aside and walked into the smokily-lighted room with its low adobe ceiling and windowless rear walls.

As he turned the older man's muddy eyes swung from the constable to Bryan Alvarado. He was still annoyed but now he was also circumspect. He knew both of his late visitors. 'I am closed,' he said, drawing himself up to his full, lean height. 'If you had come only fifteen . . .'

Sutherland broke across the flowing Spanish using English. 'Ambrosio, when was Juan Mendez here tonight?'

Garcia squinted. 'Who?'

'Juan Mendez who rides for Soledad ranch

and works for Mister Alvarado, here.'

Ambrosio Garcia's quick, sunk-set black eyes flicked to Bryan then back to Sutherland. '*That* Juan Mendez,' he said in English.

Sutherland scowled. 'Yes, that Juan Mendez.'

Garcia was a man of quick anger. 'There are many Juan Mendezes,' he said sharply. 'As many as there are John Smiths.'

Sutherland's scowl lifted but his gaze was fixed and hard. 'When was he here?'

Garcia shot Alvarado another quick look before answering. 'Early. About supper time I think.'

'What did he say, who did he talk to?'

Garcia spread his hands palms downward. 'It was a very busy night, *jefe.*'

Sutherland's expression was changing, his gaze was turning openly hostile. He did not say another word, but Ambrosio Garcia was almost seventy and had been a saloonman for about thirty of those years; he knew men, particularly the ones who were getting angry.

'Well,' he replied, speaking more clearly now, almost briskly. 'He came in late and sat at a table with old Tiburcio Velasquez. He bought drinks.' Garcia sniffed. 'Tiburcio never has any money. He sells barely enough goat milk to keep from starving.'

Sutherland looked helplessly at Alvarado, then swore at Ambrosio Garcia. 'I don't give a good gawddamn about goats. When did Juan Mendez leave and who besides Velasquez did he talk to?'

'No one as far as I know. They sat and talked for a long time then they left together. That was about two hours ago . . . Tell me, *jefe*, has something happened to Juan Mendez?'

Instead of answering Al Sutherland asked another question. 'You served them?'

Garcia nodded.

'You saw them close and often?'

Garcia was beginning to look worried as he nodded again.

Sutherland then said, 'What kind of a gun was Juan Mendez carrying?'

Garcia blinked. 'What kind? An old sixgun, the only gun I've ever seen him wear.'

'What kind of grips on it?'

Garcia stared at Sutherland as though he thought the constable was becoming simple. 'Rubber grips. The same kind everyone else has on their guns, *jefe*. Worn rubber grips with that little horse on them.'

Sutherland looked at Bryan then went to a bench and sat down studying Ambrosio Garcia. The saloonman peered from one of them to the other, thoroughly baffled.

Bryan moved over in front of Garcia and smiled. 'When was the last time you saw anyone carrying a sixgun with ivory grips?'

Garcia's bewilderment deepened. He pushed

out his hands again, palms down. 'I don't remember. In Mex-town there are a few engraved sterling silver handles.' He shrugged. 'The *machos* carry them; the young buckaroos wear them; the same roosters who wear their spurs down a notch so the rowels will turn the dirt as they walk. But no ivory grips. They cost a lot of money and silver is cheap.'

'But you have seen such guns?' Bryan asked in Spanish, and Garcia shrugged again. 'Yes. Over in *gringo*-town now and then. There is such a pistol hanging on the wall at Leland Potter's saloon.'

'Think now, friend. When was the last time you saw a man with such a pistol over in *gringo*-town?'

Garcia retreated to a bench before answering, and he frowned in concentration before finally saying, 'I think it must have been several years ago. A cowboy got drunk and there was a fight . . .'

Sutherland slapped his legs and shot up to his feet. 'That's the man Leland took the gun off of,' he told Bryan and jerked his head as he headed for the door. Ambrosio Garcia watched them walk out of his saloon with a worried, puzzled expression on his face. He went to the bar to blow out the candles over there. Outside, Alvarado saw darkness behind them where there had been light and led the way through a maze of crooked little byways toward a

particular mud residence. At his side
Sutherland said, 'Somebody is either lying or
wrong as hell. If Mendez had an ivory-handled
sixgun at the liverybarn and over here he had an
ordinary one . . .'

Bryan was watching ahead in the deeper
gloom made by little mud *jacals* for a particular
one near the outer environs of Mex-town when
he said, 'I hope to hell Velasquez knows more
than Garcia did.'

A dog barked and that awakened some goats;
they bleated. The chain reaction spread to the
flat-roofed, square mud residence and a candle
came weakly to life, visible through a glassless
window over which a blanket hung. There were
a number of small holes in the blanket.

Bryan held out his arm to stop Constable
Sutherland. From a few yards out he called
softly in Spanish. When an answer came back it
was not at the doorway, it was over along the
west side of the house where it was especially
dark. A gaunt old man with a mop of almost
pure white hair stepped into view with a carbine
in his hands. He was wearing an ancient poncho
over rumpled cotton trousers that missed
reaching his ankles by many inches. Despite his
stoop he was tall.

Bryan led the way and side-stepped as a small
dog appeared from nowhere in a snapping
lunge. The gaunt old ghost with the Winchester
snapped a command in Spanish and the dog

tucked his tail and fled in the direction of the smelly goat corral.

The old man grounded his weapon, extended a horny hand and smiled at Bryan, then looked at Constable Sutherland with his smile fading slightly.

He took them inside his house and lighted two more candles, an unprecedented extravagance, then he went to a cooler and brought back three tin cups and a jug of goat's milk. Being very poor did not appear to have broken his spirit nor inhibited his sense of hospitality.

Then he sat down looking from very black eyes straight at Bryan. Bryan put his tobacco sack and papers on the old table, then asked about his rider and the old man spoke while reaching with elaborate indifference for the sack and papers. He had been unable to afford cigarettes for many years.

'I saw him,' he told Alvarado. 'We met at the *cantina* and had a few drinks.' He rolled his cigarette with great care then leaned to puff it to life from a candle, and finally settled back savouring the taste, black eyes upon Alvarado. 'Do you want to know about the gun or where he is now?'

Al Sutherland leaned forward from his seat at the table watching the old man's strong features and serene expression. 'Both,' he said quietly and for the first time Velasquez looked directly

73

at the lawman for any length of time. He pulled down another lungful of smoke then arose without a word and went to grope down inside a large wooden box. When he returned to the table he put a blued Colt sixgun with ivory grips on the table. Sutherland reached for the weapon as the old man spoke directly to Bryan Alvarado. 'He gave it to me. He said I could sell it for a lot of money . . . He had it in his belt in back, under his jacket and did not show it to me until we came up here to drink some goat milk.' The black eyes went to the gun Sutherland was turning over in his hands. 'It has been fired hasn't it?'

Sutherland nodded without looking up, then he placed the gun on the table in front of Bryan and raised his eyes to the old man's face. 'Where did he get it?'

The old man met Sutherland's gaze easily and when he replied it was not to answer Sutherland's question it was to ask one of his own. 'Do you recognise that gun, *jefe?*'

Sutherland smiled a little. Beside him Bryan Alvarado was examining the gun. 'I've seen it a hundred times, friend,' Sutherland replied in Spanish. 'Have you seen it before?'

Velasquez also half-smiled. 'Not that many times, *jefe*. Even if I had money to buy whisky with I would not go to Potter's saloon. He won't serve—beaners.'

'How did Juan Mendez get hold of it,

friend?'

'A rider dropped it. Juan was loping into town. Someone was out there west of town riding southward in a great hurry and did not see Juan even when they almost ran into each other. Juan yelled and the other man was so startled he yanked his horse hard around; the horse stumbled, went to his knees and would have fallen if the man had not pulled him back upright. Then the man spurred wildly southward in a run, and Juan sat watching for a while and was about to ride on when he saw something white on the ground.' Velasquez pointed to the gun in Alvarado's hands.

CHAPTER EIGHT

A SIGHT TO REMEMBER

They left Mex-town by picking their way carefully among the little crooked byways and emerged onto the plankwalk in front of the general store. Al Sutherland led the way to his jailhouse office and lighted a lamp before going behind his desk to drop into the chair and look at his companion. They had left the gun with Tiburcio Velasquez and had heard from him that Juan Mendez had not told the old man where he was going after he left Velasquez.

75

Sutherland hit the desk-top with a big balled fist. 'Hell, I should have quessed. Lee never goes out without a hat. The top of his head sunburns where the hair used to be.'

Alvarado went to stand in front of the stove. 'A lot of people wear hats,' he said absently, thinking about Juan Mendez. Without much doubt Mendez had recognised that gun. Why he had put it into his holster instead of his waistband after picking it up was something only Juan could answer, and right now that was not important anyway. Alvarado glanced at the constable. 'Why should Leland Potter be riding south in the night?'

Sutherland leaned back making his chair squeak. 'You can make as good a guess as I can. Maybe because he knows someone is looking for him. Maybe to get his friends the border-jumpers to get up here in a hurry, before the town knows what's coming and gets prepared.' Sutherland wagged his head. 'It's hard to believe. I've known Lee Potter for a long time. He sells good whisky. This is the first time I've ever . . .'

'Come along,' Bryan said abruptly, crossing toward the door. It had just occurred to him where he might find Juan Mendez.

There was a chill in the night as they crossed the dark, empty roadway and walked northward in the direction of the saloon. As they got closer Bryan squinted at the building. 'If Potter has to

76

go all the way down to some gourd-town to fetch his friends back with him, we'll have plenty of time.'

Sutherland did not say a word until they were around behind the saloon picking their way through debris and had the rear door in sight. Then he halted and raised a thick arm. The door was ajar.

Bryan let go a pent-up breath of relief. He had been right over at the jailhouse; he knew where Juan Mendez was. But they approached the door soundlessly and halted, one on each side as Bryan leaned to call softly into the pitch blackness of the building.

'Juan! . . . Juan, it's Bryan. Do you hear me?'

There was no answer. In fact there was not a sound of any kind beyond the ajar door.

Bryan palmed his sixgun and tried again. 'Juan! We talked to Tiburcio . . . Do you hear me?'

This time there was a sound. Not an answer but a whispery sound of movement in the darkness beyond the door. The whispery sound ended and someone cocked a gun; that sound carried perfectly.

Al Sutherland also drew his sixgun. He was flat against the wall looking over at Bryan with a dark scowl.

Bryan's palm was wet around the pistol-grip. He leaned again and this time raised his voice slightly. 'Juan! We know who it was who dropped the sixgun you picked up. Al Sutherland is out here with me . . . Open the door.'

A carbine barrel appeared around the door, came to rest against wood and moved back taking the door inward with it. Sutherland and Alvarado pulled back and flattened, guns raised. A quiet voice said, 'Who else beside the constable?'

'No one,' stated Bryan.

'. . . Come inside and stop.'

They obeyed. It was not possible to see Juan Mendez. He was behind some wooden crates. The only thing they could see very well was light reflecting from somewhere down the barrel of his saddlegun. Then the gun dropped down and a thin shadow emerged from behind the crates and walked closer. Mendez squinted at his employer. 'I been wondering how I was going to get you into town without making the ride myself.' Mendez stared at the constable. 'Put up the guns,' he said. 'Follow me. Be careful. This is the storeroom, it's full of crates with bottles in them and broken furniture.'

Sutherland bumped something unyielding and swore under his breath. 'Light a damned candle,' he exclaimed.

Mendez was in a doorway and turned. 'No. Feel your way.'

That is what they did, but once clear of the

storeroom it was a little lighter because starlight was coming through the front-wall windows.

Mendez moved more briskly now, going along the narrow place behind the bar with quick steps. He emerged at the south end of the bar and looked over his shoulders to be sure Alvarado and Sutherland were behind him, then he moved without any hesitation past some poker tables with chairs atop them and halted where an old curtain hung in front of a door. He held the curtain for them, and finally there was candle-light.

The room they entered was fairly large with framed pictures on the walls, a large bed in a corner near a carved oak dresser with a round mirror above it. A closet door hung open showing clothes and some boxes. Mendez crossed to the door and looked back. 'Through here. Push the clothes aside.'

There was a small door cut into the rear wall of the closet and as long as clothing was hanging there it was invisible. It was the clothing that made the closet look like every other clothes-closet.

Mendez pushed through the hanging attire and disappeared through the small door. Bryan was behind him and when he straightened up in candle-light he was in a small windowless room full of stale air and carefully stacked crates. Four of those crates he recognised at once as belonging to a stage company. They were bullion boxes, reinforced at each corner with steel plates, and their hinged tops were also reinforced with steel.

Constable Sutherland had to suck in his stomach to make it through the little doorway. When he straightened up and looked around, his expelled breath sounded unusually loud.

Juan Mendez approached a bullion box which had been placed on a small table. The lid was lying back. When Bryan walked over Juan reached in and brought a heavy object out of the box which he held close to the candle. It was a massive gold crucifix with blood-red rubies and dazzling green emeralds set in it.

Sutherland leaned on the little table staring. Slowly he turned to look into the bullion box. It was two-thirds full of other objects made of gold, all of them with a religious significance.

Juan replaced the crucifix and tapped Bryan's arm as he pointed to the piled boxes. 'Full of loot,' he said quietly. 'I never saw so much gold in my life. Most of it has the Mexican eagle-serpent insignia stamped on it.' Juan waved his arm around the little room. In a voice made soft by awe he said, 'I forgot the time. When you called I thought it was Potter; I thought he'd come back.'

Sutherland lifted several of the boxes and had to grunt despite his size and strength, then he sat down atop one of the boxes looking at Mendez and Alvarado, momentarily stunned.

'My gawd . . . how long's Leland been doing this? There's a fortune here. It's hard to believe even when you're lookin' at it . . . Bryan?'

Bryan was turning slowly, taking in the sight of all those crates and having as hard a time accepting what he saw as the lawman'd had. Finally he faced his rider. 'Why didn't you hunt up the constable?'

Mendez looked squarely at his employer. 'If Leland Potter the saloonman in town was doing this, how could I know he didn't have partners? I was getting ready to take some of it back with me to the ranch to show you.' Juan went to sit down before continuing. 'Tiburcio suspected something. A few times when he couldn't sleep and went outside to his corral he saw horsemen riding silently southward from Mex-town. At first he thought it was *vaqueros* from town who worked at the ranches going away to work. But twice he saw a *gringo* meet the *vaqueros* and take them behind Mex-town out of sight. Tiburcio said he followed them on foot one time but was afraid to do it again. They were standing out there talking. He couldn't get close enough to hear what they were saying, but he saw the Mexicans ride away southward and the *gringo* go back through Mex-town up through a dog-trot. He was afraid to get close enough for a good look but he said the *gringo* was nearly bald. Tiburcio said for a long time he tried to remember what it was about the *gringo* that troubled him. He was sure he had seen him before.' Juan shrugged thin shoulders. 'Tonight when I showed him the gun he remembered why that man had seemed familiar to him. It had been Leland Potter.'

Alvarado sat leaning loosely forward. The last time he and Potter had talked had been when the guards had been shot off the high seat of the prison wagon and the men inside had been set free. Leland had told Bryan and Frank all about it, and had leaned against his bar looking pleased that he knew something his customers had not heard before.

Potter was more than just extremely clever, he was also one hell of a good actor.

Sutherland gazed dumbly around. 'We been friends for years. Lee's a likeable man . . . Hell, I used to tease him about those cigars he chewed and never lit. I wish I had a dollar for every time we sat around on winter nights playing cards.' Sutherland arose. 'This is going to upset the town more'n the story about raiders coming up here.'

Mendez took the candle with him as they left the little secret room and made their way back into the bar-room from Potter's living quarters. There, Sutherland halted, reached for a bottle, filled three glasses and picked up one of them. He was the hardest hit of them all. Mendez and Bryan Alvarado had been concerned only with the extent of Potter's hoard, the town constable had initially been stunned by that too, but now he was thinking of his friend of many years who was responsible for encouraging border-jumpers to murder, burn towns, rob churches so that he could pay a probable pittance for the loot.

They left the glasses atop the bar and returned to the dark alleyway, and startled a big, slab-sided bony-tailed dog who had been foraging among the rubbish. The dog fled, running as hard as he could.

Without a word they went over to the jailhouse where Constable Sutherland stirred up a fire in his office stove and placed a graniteware coffeepot atop it. He moved and acted fifteen years older than he was.

Alvarado looked at his rider. 'How did you find the little room?'

Mendez answered off-handedly. 'I knew he probably wouldn't be back until some time tomorrow, so I started out just looking. It was not hard to find when I pushed those clothes aside. I used a hunting knife I found in a bedside-drawer to break the lock open.'

Sutherland came out of his reverie. 'Why did you put that fancy gun in your holster when you rode into town?'

Mendez looked slightly embarrassed. 'It was a much better one than my gun. I just wanted to see what it would feel like to have a gun like that in my holster.'

Sutherland went to see if the coffee was hot.

It was not hot but it was warm so he filled three cups and passed two of them around then returned to his desk to hunch over the third cup. 'In the morning I'll put armed men inside the saloon to guard the place . . . Hell; what am I goin' to do with all that stuff?'

Bryan answered matter-of-factly. 'Get some Mex officials up here, maybe some churchmen, and let them identify it and take it back where it belongs.'

Sutherland's eyes narrowed. 'You got any idea what'll happen if word gets out how much wealth is in that little room? I'll have outlaws comin' in here by the dozen.'

'Don't say anything about it,' replied Alvarado. 'At least not until you've contacted the Mex Authorities. You couldn't keep it a secret forever anyway, Al . . . What worries me right now isn't the cache. Lee Potter knows he lost that fancy gun and he won't have to think about it for very long to know that whoever finds the thing will recognise it as the gun he's had on display in the saloon for two or three years. Whether he guesses the rest of it—that we've connected him with the border-jumpers—or not, if he figures to bring them back up here to raid the town, maybe burn it and kill a lot of people, my guess is that he's ready to pull out of the Valverde country anyway . . . Hell, he's got more gold in his hideout than ten men could spend the rest of their lives if they lived to be a hundred and fifty. Why should he stay here running a saloon?' Bryan stood up. 'Al, I don't think Lee aims to leave much behind when he finishes with this town . . . Come on, Juan; if we hurry we can get home before Jinglebob throws it out.'

CHAPTER NINE

RIDERS!

Not a word was said when Bryan and Juan Mendez crossed to the cookhouse after caring for their horses and walked in. The men were at breakfast and they paused to glance up. Jinglebob looked irritably at the new arrivals, moved his lips in silent grumbling and got ready to feed two more. It was not having to do this that annoyed him; when it had been discovered earlier that Juan and Bryan were not around, the men wondered, worried, and speculated. Jinglebob had gone right along with the rest of them even though in the back of his mind he had been sure he had seen Bryan leave the yard last night in the company of someone he thought was Constable Sutherland. What irritated him was that Bryan had not told anyone he was going to ride out last night.

As Jinglebob was placing their coffee cups on the table he said, 'Well, it's nice to have you gents back,' and looked sourly at his employer.

Bryan talked as he ate. He told them where Juan had gone and what he'd wanted to find out. He told them about Ambrosio Garcia and old Tiburcio Velasquez. Finally he told them what Juan had found in that hidden room.

It was so much like a story of suspense the men sat and listened without moving until the recitation was finished, then big Jim Fisk went after the coffee pot, topped up his cup and shoved the pot along the table in case anyone else needed a re-fill. He said, 'Potter'd do something like that.' The others looked at him. Jim was unabashed. 'I've had a feelin' about him for a long time. Yeah I know, he's friendly and all but I've still had a feelin' about him.' Jim let it stop there and reached for his cup.

Frank Miller was not as interested in the saloonman as he was in the hoard. 'Sutherland better put some real trustworthy men to guarding that stuff. Real trustworthy.'

Poker Flannery rolled a smoke as he said, 'If he rode down yonder to round up his friends,' Poker paused to light up and trickle smoke. 'I got an idea Sutherland would do well to send someone among the outlyin' ranches, because he might need all the help he can get.'

'The army,' exclaimed Jinglebob. 'With artillery and cavalry.'

No one responded to that. Bryan rose and spoke to Juan. 'You better get some rest.' He got as far as the door before Frank called. 'What are we to do, just sit here?'

'I'll let you know in a couple of hours,' he replied and left the cookhouse, tired all the way through.

While Bryan slept fully clothed except for his boots, hat and gunbelt, the men at the bunkhouse queried Juan, and when he finally left them with their smokes and coffee heading for his bunk, Poker Flannery gazed at Jim Fisk with a tough look tinged with dry humour. 'When I went to work for Soledad years back folks told me it wouldn't be like most other places I've rode for.'

Frank Miller re-filled his cup, grinning. 'Let that be a lesson to you,' he said, and tasted the coffee. It was not even warm and left an acidy taste in his mouth. He got up and jerked his head. 'We can cuff horses and dung out the barn until Bryan's caught up on his sleep.'

They were crossing the yard in fresh sunlight when Frank stopped. 'Suppose Sutherland don't put some scouts out?'

Jim and Poker considered this briefly. 'He'll do that,' stated Jim, starting forward again. 'Anybody'd have sense enough to do that. Besides, Potter can't get back up here with his cut-throats until maybe tomorrow, at the soonest.'

'There'll be hell to pay in town,' Frank mused, entering the barn behind Jim.

No one disputed this. They got shanks and went out back to bring in their animals. As they were tying them outside the harness-room Frank had something to add to his other remarks. 'What about our horses those sons of bitches stole?'

Poker had no illusions on that score. 'Down in Messico by now. If Potter's *pistoleros* happen to be riding some of them maybe we can at least get those back . . . Where's the army, Frank?'

The rangeboss could only guess. 'Riding patrol, escorting wagons. Maybe down at some of those gourd-towns that got raided settin' things to rights.'

'Yeah,' Poker grunted. 'If I was Sutherland I'd have riders flaggin' it down-country to round them up.'

Frank had something different in mind today from what they were doing. Some of the Soledad horses had been deliberately scattered by the fleeing fugitives. They would probably be somewhere on the range. It had been his intention when he had rolled out this morning to go looking for them, bring them back to the corrals so they would all have a change of saddle-stock.

He was not interested in the army. Experience had taught him that down along the border army patrols had all they could do pursuing raiders from below the line. They rarely responded to someone's notion that a town was to be raided, perhaps because those rumours were a penny a dozen and almost never proved to be true.

The sun was climbing, Jinglebob came to loiter in the barn to take part in the desultory conversations, but mostly to talk about the hoard of stolen wealth. It had soaked in slowly, as most things had throughout Jinglebob's long life, but this time when the full import was comprehensible, the old rider-turned-cook seemed obsessed with all that wealth. He probably had never heard of such a vast hoard before, let alone talked to men who had actually seen and touched it.

He mentioned all the things that could be accomplished after the gold and jewels were broken down for sale. He even dredged up a dream of his he had not thought about lately but which in his earlier life he had thought about a lot.

A nice foothill cow ranch with a southern exposure to guarantee first grass. Thousands of acres with creeks and timber, a decent log house and maybe even a wife.

Jim and Poker brought in another pair of horses to be curried and looked over. Jinglebob, sitting on an empty horseshoe keg, had not even missed them. He was still talking when someone in the yard called out. Everyone's attention was caught by the shout and something urgent in it. The younger men dropped their brushes and went swiftly past old Jinglebob. He came out of his reverie slowly, struggled up to his feet and also headed for the yard.

Juan Mendez was standing between the bunkhouse and barn, facing southwesterly, his body tense and leaning slightly. Poker and Jim almost reached him when Juan flashed a glance over at them and raised an arm to point.

There were horsemen coming toward the yard from a considerable distance and as they loped forward they spread out. This brought a startled cry from old Jinglebob who had arrived over close to the bunkhouse as the riders were executing this manoeuvre.

He said, 'Skirmish order,' then went scuttling toward the main-house for Bryan.

Jim swore and ran into the bunkhouse for his weapons. Like most rangemen, Fisk did not even wear a belt-gun while engaged in routine ranch work.

Frank and Poker jostled past Jim as they also ran inside for their weapons and when they returned to the yard Bryan was on the porch of his main-house with Jinglebob. The *cocinero* was speaking volubly and rapidly and Bryan was ignoring him as he watched the approaching horsemen.

He ducked back inside and re-appeared

almost instantly with his gunbelt and Winchester. He paused on the porch to buckle the belt into place then told Jinglebob to come with him and went down to join the other men near the bunkhouse.

Frank Miller was calm when he looked around at his employer and said, 'Mexicans.'

Bryan counted the horsemen. There were fourteen of them. He pulled his hat down in front and scowled. If they were riding to attack his yard it made no sense. His ranch was not the only cow outfit in the Valverde country nor even the closest one to town.

Poker said, 'Crazy. There's no cover between them and the yard.'

Bryan had a spy-glass in the house but made no move to get it. The riders were not coming in a run, they were instead riding at an easy lope. Jinglebob went scuttling in the direction of the cookshack and when Frank and Bryan turned in that direction moments later in response to the sound of a door slamming, old Jinglebob was on the porch with a long-barrelled rifle, a Winchester saddlegun, and was frantically trying to buckle a shellbelt around his middle and keep an eye upon the approaching Mexicans at the same time.

He got the belt secured, adjusted the holstered Colt, leaned to pick up the old long-barrelled rifle and was in the act of raising it to his shoulder when Bryan yelled at him.

'Put it down! Jinglebob! *Put that damned rifle down!*'

The older man lowered it just enough to call back. 'I got better range; I can hit 'em from here.'

Bryan swore. 'You put that gun down—right now!'

Jinglebob obeyed slowly, squinting in Alvarado's direction as though he suspected his employer had lost his wits. 'It's Messicans, for Chris'sake,' he yelled. 'Ridin' in skirmish order.'

That much was the truth but what had inspired Bryan to stop his cook from firing on the horsemen was the way they were heading in; not fast, with no weapons in hand, and sitting straight up in their saddles.

It dawned on the three rangemen standing with Bryan that something was not quite right, if this was an attack. Jim Fisk turned, spat aside, turned back and said, 'Frank . . . ?'

The rangeboss was straining to make out individual riders. They were close enough now for that. He said, 'Jim, two of the closest ones are from Mex-town. That 'possum-bellied one—I forget his name—he worked at the corralyard for a long time.'

A gaunt rider with thick grey hair who was riding a dappled horse removed his hat at sight of the bunched men in the yard and waved vigorously. He yelled something in Spanish which the men in the yard could not distinguish, then crushed his hat back down and continued to lope ahead with his arm raised.

Frank and Bryan exchanged a puzzled frown. Jim Fisk jettisoned his cud of tobacco and ran a large hand across his lips. 'That's the old goat-man out in front, Bryan. I've seen him a dozen times driving his goats over east of town.'

Juan sighed. 'Tiburcio,' he said without taking his eyes off the old man riding toward the yard still with his arm raised. Juan turned toward Bryan. 'Somethin' is wrong as hell.'

The riders were within a hundred and fifty yards of the barn and corrals, their sound strong and echoless in the silence of the yard, when another sound, deeper, like a shattering of the atmosphere, rather like thunder but not that high in the air, came from the opposite direction causing the stationary range men to turn. Waves of faint reverberation washed over them.

Juan Mendez swung back toward the riders and raised his fist with the Winchester in it, then hurried in the direction of the corrals where the riders were converging.

Tiburcio Velasquez came down off his mount with surprising suppleness considering his age. The other Mexicans came up stirring clouds of dust.

Bryan led his riders over there as old

Velasquez raised his mahogany-coloured gaunt old face and showed fiery black eyes.

'We were watching,' he yelled above the rattle of men and horses around him. '*El Jefe* made up two parties of us, one to ride southward to the east of town, the other party to go west.' Velasquez paused to breathe hard for a moment, clearly very agitated. 'He said we would only have to keep watch until afternoon then other men from town would take over from us . . .'

Three heavy-set Mexicans with sweat dripping from their chins pushed through carrying something. They stopped in front of Bryan and dropped whatever they had been carrying. It was a dead man.

One of the other Mexicans spoke up in English. 'This was one of their scouts. He saw us and tried to turn back south. We cut him off so he ran west . . . We caught up and shot him.'

The Soledad men gazed downward. The dead man was a *bandelero*. He was wearing two sixguns and one of them was still under a tie-thong in its holster.

Bryan raised his head slowly. 'Scouts?' he said to Velasquez and a lank, tall younger man walked up beside old Tiburcio. 'It was said in Mex-town last night that they would reach Valverde this morning.'

'Who the hell are "they"?' Jim Fisk growled.

The tall Mexican spread his hands. '*El patron* of the *bandeleros* and his raiders.'

Jim was incredulous. 'Leland Potter?' Even as he said this he turned a crooked scowl toward Bryan. 'You said they couldn't get up for another day or two.'

Bryan pointed at the dead man. 'He could answer you, Jim, I can't.' As he dropped the arm back to his side he and Tiburcio Velasquez exchanged a look. The old man spoke in Spanish.

'We do not know how many or how they got up here so quickly, but we know why they are here. Everyone in Mex-town knew that yesterday; to burn down Valverde and plunder it and kill everyone they can find. We will give you the dead bandit and we will go back now.' Tiburcio turned and called gruffly in Spanish. His men pulled their animals around to be mounted.

Bryan called to his riders. They raced for the barn. One of the Valverde Mexicans yelled something as he and others raced across the yard riding eastward. The man grinned through sweat and raised his carbine.

Bryan and the others worked fast. There were questions but no one asked them. Only as they were pulling the horses out front to be mounted did Frank Miller ask how it could be Potter's border-jumpers if he'd had to go all the way down to the border to round them up

95

before heading back?

Frank was of the opinion it was another band of marauders from Mexico. If that were so, then Valverde was in even greater danger because Potter might arrive with his men to support the men who were now attacking the town.

Poker was riding stirrup with Bryan when he said, 'Potter maybe didn't have to ride down to the border, Bryan. Maybe his renegades were on the way up here when he met them.'

That was a strong possibility. Bryan did not comment on it because someone behind him a few yards called out and Bryan turned in the saddle. Far back coming through the dust with elbows flapping, one hand full of reins the other hand holding a long-barrelled rifle, was the *cocinero*.

This time no one was going to leave Jinglebob behind!

They did not see the Mex-town horsemen again although they rode through their dust all the way. No one said anything when Jinglebob eventually caught up and rode among them, weathered, lined old face twisted with concentration and belligerence. In his bitterness there was room for just one thought: If the others had done nothing so far toward avenging Jake Monroe, *he* would!

They heard gunfire from a considerable distance west of Valverde but it was sporadic, not in volleys as they had expected it would be.

They were less than a mile out with dust obscuring things up ahead when another of those shuddering, reverberating blasts of air beat against them but this time they were close enough to hear the explosion. It almost stampeded their horses.

They could also see a huge gout of dirt and dust rise into the air over Valverde immediately after the explosion. Jinglebob yelled above the noise. 'Cannon! The bastards got a cannon with 'em!'

It was not true but it was a reasonable assumption.

CHAPTER TEN

GUNS AND DUST

No one challenged them. They reached the back alley behind the liverybarn and did not meet a soul although an occasional shout or a gunshot sounded up the roadway.

There was no one to care for their animals so they did it themselves, stalling the horses and leaving their outfits up-ended in front of stall doors.

Bryan went up front and leaned to peer outward. The lower end of Valverde seemed deserted. There was dust hanging over town

97

from the harness shop northward. There was a large hole in the centre of the roadway. Someone sang out in guttural border-Spanish and got back some laughter.

The riders walked up cautiously, did not expose anything but their heads and also looked up the roadway. Jinglebob sounded disgusted when he said, 'Drunk. Drunk and crazy. They never got no science when they attack a place. Worse'n In'ians.'

Bryan led the way down through the runway into the alley. It was empty and although there was dust northward at this lower end of town the same impression of desertion or abandonment prevailed.

He was going to lead his crew northward when a brisk exchange of gunfire erupted around on Main Street somewhere. When it ended they left the barn, went to the opposite side of the alley and began working their way northward, each man responsible for himself. Only one of them had been in a battle before and none of them, with the exception of old Jinglebob, had ever been a soldier. Jinglebob acted as though he had been through something like this. In fact when they were among the chicken houses and buggy sheds opposite the abstract office he signalled for Bryan to wait, to move into deeper cover and wait.

Bryan obeyed. They all did. Another wild exchange of gunfire erupted and this time there were hooting shouts accompanying it.

Jinglebob hovered, rifle up across his body in both hands, then dashed across the empty alley and got flat alongside the wall of the abstract office. Nothing happened, but someone was yelling in gravelly Spanish, which they could not understand because there were some sporadic carbine shots and more of the derisive, hooting noise made by men who scorned their adversaries.

Bryan saw swift movement from the corner of his eye. Frank also saw it and knelt beside a dilapidated old carriage shed, raising his Winchester carefully. But whatever had caused that movement did not show itself. For all Frank and Bryan knew it could have been a frightened dog. Valverde had its share of dogs.

Jinglebob gave an imperious jerk of his head to summon the others across the alley and as they darted over there one at a time Jinglebob knelt, rifle to shoulder, to give them cover.

Poker Flannery ended up slightly breathless beside the *cocinero* and eyed him closely. Jinglebob knew what he was doing, which Poker didn't.

He waited in that kneeling position until he was satisfied about something, then raised the rifle, took long aim, and shot the latch off the rear door of the abstract office. Then he snapped at the others and raced over, kicked the door open and sprang inside.

Bryan and Jim Fisk exchanged a look, then also ran along the back of the building and through the doorway.

Jinglebob was along the front wall, close to the wall where two windows had had the panes of glass shot out. The office was empty and smelled of dynamite. Some of the furniture had scars to indicate that bullets had come inward from out front.

Frank eased over to Bryan and said, 'Where the hell is Sutherland? Where are the townsmen he should have had waitin' for those bastards?'

Bryan did not reply because he had nothing to say. Right now he had led his riders into a genuine battle, and although it had been almost too easy to get in here, from the sounds, the dust, the smell of explosives and the close-up gunfire which seemed to erupt in spurts, Bryan was worried about how they could get back out of Valverde if they had to.

Poker knelt back in the centre of the room in order to be able to skyline the rooftops across the road. But there were no marauders up there.

Jinglebob squatted, edged up to the window, placed his rifle barrel upon the wooden sill and waited. When nothing happened he sprang around, stared hard, then sprang back.

The other men approached the roadside wall. Jinglebob called something but again gunfire drowned him out, and this time it was fierce

100

and sustained. Someone was firing from the buildings adjacent to the abstract office. It was a steady, stationary fire. Across the road and beyond that big hole in the roadway, the men firing back moved constantly. Their shots never appeared to come from the same direction twice. But Bryan noticed they were always in the vicinity of the saloon, either around in the west-side alley or among the other buildings with shattered windows adjacent to the saloon. He leaned toward his rangeboss. 'They're not trying to plunder the stores, Frank.'

Miller nodded grimly. 'Whoever's in the buildings north of us's got 'em pinned down.'

Bryan shook his head but did not argue. He crawled closer to the front wall and, perhaps because up until now the raiders had had no reason to look in the direction of the abstract office and were being kept busy northward, he and his riders could hunker below the sills and peer out.

Juan Mendez was shading his eyes from sunlight being reflected off thick dust when he suddenly said, 'There is a wagon over there.' He swung to stare at Bryan. 'That's why they're not moving away from the saloon . . . They're giving Potter protection while he loads his bullion crates in the wagon.'

Poker Flannery went to the rear door and peeked out to the left and right and someone yelled at him in English. He sucked back as though he'd been shot. The yelling man continued to call. Poker looked up where his companions were and rolled his eyes; that man could have blown his head off.

Bryan went back there. The yelling had stopped but the moment Bryan pushed his carbine barrel out and wig-wagged with it the shouting began again.

Bryan grounded his Winchester. 'Al Sutherland,' he told Poker, and leaned, cupped both hands and yelled back. 'Can you make it over here?'

There was no answer but moments later the big town constable appeared sprinting hard, and this time there was someone else in the alley. They shot wildly the first time but as the constable came hurtling through the wide-open door the second bullet was so close he felt roiled air at the back of his neck.

Poker slammed and barred the door.

Sutherland's clothing was filthy and torn, his face was shiny and red. He waited a moment to recover his breath then wagged his head. 'They blew open the bank. That was the first anyone knew they had arrived. Blew it open then started shooting at people who rushed out of stores to see what the explosion was about . . . Bryan, I had scouts out all around. They were already in Mex-town. They slipped over here and hell it was a war before we knew what was happening.'

Bryan nodded. 'Is Leland with them?'

'With them, for Chris-sake! Lee's directing them. I think he's loadin' a wagon with his loot from that little room.'

'Where are the townsmen, Al?'

Sutherland squinted toward the dusty sunshine and let his voice drop a couple of notches. 'Scairt and disorganised. I didn't have time to call that meetin' at the fire-house.'

Bryan studied the constable. Along with being badly upset Sutherland right at this moment would not meet Bryan's gaze. He had said he did not want to call the meeting; maybe that was part of the reason the town had been surprised.

Frank turned and beckoned from his hunkering position. They crossed cautiously toward the front of the office. It was possible now and then to see men darting away from the back of the saloon, rushing southward toward the rear of the other stores over there.

No one understood what this signified until Jinglebob made a gagging sound and ducked low to pull back the butt-plate of his rifle, hold steady briefly, then squeeze off a shot that nearly deafened the men in the room with him. They all jumped clear of the window and Jinglebob rolled sideways to flatten out of harm's way.

He saw the others staring at him and jerked a thumb. 'I glimpsed a team an' wagon goin' north between the back of the saloon an' the gunsmith's place—through the dog-trot. I waited for the seat to appear an' shot at the man settin' up there.'

Someone had seen the black-powder smoke and now fired a ranging shot past the glassless window. It holed a blue coffeepot atop the office stove.

Bryan saw Poker leaning gingerly to fire beyond the window and was yelling at him when another bullet came through and blood poured. Poker dropped his carbine, clapped a hand to one side of his head and sprang away.

They waited for him to collapse. The left shoulder of his shirt was scarlet. More blood trickled past his fingers, his face was contorted. Bryan and the constable reached him and forced his hand away to examine the wound. There was a notch out of the middle portion of Poker's left ear. They cut some cloth and wrapped his head. The blood soaked through. Sutherland told him to hold another cloth tightly to the side of his head, very tightly, and that seemed to prevent most of the bleeding.

Poker was fighting mad. He did not appear to be in any pain as he tried to retrieve his Winchester with one hand while holding the side of his head with the other hand.

Juan Mendez called and gestured. Opposite the abstract office there were marauders inside the general store. They were plundering. Frank

104

and Jinglebob knelt beside Juan, placed their weapons across wood for steadiness then waited. Two Mexicans with crossed shell-belts over their chests had found the clothing. They flung shirts and trousers in all directions until they found something they liked, then started toward the glass case which held new handguns.

One raider kicked out the glass. Juan said, 'Now!' and aimed, held his breath and fired. Frank and Jinglebob also fired. Both raiders dropped like stones.

The Soledad riders dropped and frantically rolled, but there was no volley of return fire. Two shots came, one from up near the saloon, the other one from farther southward down the roadway, but that was all.

Bryan turned to Constable Sutherland. 'If that's Potter's wagon . . .'

Sutherland nodded. They got to the rear doorway before Frank called at them. Bryan yelled back then he and Sutherland peeked out. A bullet splintered wood within inches of the lawman's face. He sprang back so suddenly he nearly fell. Bryan saw a thick Mexican arise out of some weeds across the alley, aim a handgun at something directly in front of him and lower, and pull the trigger.

A *bandelero* sprang into the air and flopped back into the weeds. The thick Mexican grinned widely toward Bryan and held up four fingers, then he too dropped into the weeds where it was impossible to see him.

They got out of the abstract office and ran for shelter to the adjoining southward building. They continued to do this all the way to the lower end of town, and the last time they darted it was up the liverybarn runway. No one challenged them. The south end of Valverde still appeared to be free of attackers. It also appeared to be free of everyone else.

The horses were circling inside the corrals in panic. Even the animals in the barn were edgy. Bryan was tugging a stall-latch when a savage gunfight erupted over in the vicinity of the west-side alley. He paused to listen briefly then opened the door for his horse.

Constable Sutherland had trouble with his animal. That savage battle did not diminish and the horse would have hurled himself backwards and fled in terror if he'd had anyone smaller than Sutherland on the other end of the rope.

Even so he fidgeted throughout the saddling process, Sutherland's face got redder and redder until he was finished and had the reins in his hand, then he hauled the horse around and booted it squarely in the rear. The horse jumped, struggled, swung to face his exasperated owner, and stopped fidgeting.

Bryan was leading his horse toward the rear barn opening when two townsmen ran inside from out back, saw two men leading horses and flung up their weapons. Sutherland, whose mood was not the best, bawled at them. 'Carl! Jenkins! Point those guns in some other direction—you pair of damned idiots!'

The townsmen obeyed. One of them spoke in a staccato burst of nervous sound. 'Constable! It's Lee Potter! Them beaners wasn't breakin' into the saloon, they was stayin' down there until Lee got some boxes into a wagon and drove north. Constable! He was with 'em! S'help me gawd Lee Potter was with them raiders!'

Bryan went to the doorway and looked both ways, jerked his head at Al Sutherland, swung into the saddle and gigged his mount straight ahead across the alley and out into the grass-country west of town. By the time the constable joined him a mile out, there was another savage gunfight in progress over on the east side of town somewhere. When Bryan reined northward Sutherland turned beside him and said, 'That's coming from Mex-town.'

Bryan squinted through the dust which was hanging over Valverde. He could barely discern three wildly riding horsemen speeding southeastward from town. Two were hatless but beyond that he could not make out very much about them.

CHAPTER ELEVEN

DEAD MEN

They saw the wagon about the same time some outriders with it saw them. Sutherland ignored the five Mexicans who were coming around to face Alvarado and Sutherland. 'There's that damned new beaver-belly hat,' he called.

Bryan had seen the hat on the man larruping his team into a big circling run. The only other item he would have needed to know who was driving that wagon was the ivory-handled Colt in Tiburcio Velasquez's *jacal*.

Potter was standing with feet apart and legs braced as he brought the team around. What surprised Bryan was that Leland Potter the saloonman was an expert teamster. Of course the wagon was loaded but even so unless a man knew just how close he could snub a team in a turn he would roll the wagon. As it was there were moments when both off-side wheels barely touched the ground.

The outriders held a position between Sutherland and Alvarado beside the wagon. They had guns and were clearly waiting for the two oncoming horsemen to get within their range.

Potter's wagon struck a half-submerged large

rock on the off-side and nearly overturned. He eased up on the lines so the horses would head out in a straight course. For moments the wagon swayed drunkenly then settled back down. Bryan wagged his head. The devil deserved his due; Leland Potter was a very good teamster.

Al Sutherland was holding his horse to a slow lope. He knew what the outriders were waiting for and had no intention of obliging them. Once he took his eyes off the wagon and its protecting horsemen long enough to yell over to Bryan.

'I'd give a hundred dollars right now for that damned old long-barrel rifle your cook was using.' A man had to be dead serious to make that kind of a suggestion when he did not make one hundred dollars until he had worked two and a half months.

They kept their distance, the outriders had to twist rearward in their saddles to watch them because now Potter was heading straight south. Clearly, his intention was to either get down across the border, or get back to one of the gourd-towns where other *bandeleros* or their friends would provide him with protection.

Bryan studied the wagon and its mounted guard, then squinted in the direction of the sun. Finally he eased up and allowed his horse to take a slow gait. There was open country for miles; no shelter for mounted men until they were many miles southward then there were thick stands of thorny underbrush.

Potter eased up too, still driving Roman-style. He called to one of the outriders and the man swerved close. Potter told him something and as the Mexican reined away he was nodding his head.

Moments later three of the raiders slackened their gait, swerved to get behind the wagon, directly in the path of Alvarado and Sutherland, and let their horses walk. The riders had carbines in their laps and were sitting sideways looking back.

The wagon and the remaining two Mexicans picked up the pace again, gradually widening the distance. Al Sutherland said a contemptuous word.

He shortened his reins and pulled his hat down in front, then leaned slightly as he called to Bryan, 'Let's have at 'em.'

As Sutherland yelled that he swung wide to the left, drew his handgun and swung widely to the right as he booted the horse over into a run. Alvarado said 'estupido,' under his breath and gigged his mount. He crossed paths with Sutherland as they raced toward the three outriders, who finally had to halt to turn to face the charging men.

They were constantly changing course as they sped directly at the Mexicans, who had finally got their horses fully around. One of them raised a carbine and fired. He missed because

110

both Alvarado and Sutherland were bending back from the end of one of their direct runs. He levered up to fire again and one of his companions fired too. His shot was even wider of the racing, zig-zagging targets.

Sutherland was low over his horse's neck, sixgun pushed ahead. Alvarado could not see his face but he could sense the large man's intention. They only had a short distance to cover then they would be within handgun range.

The Mexicans were anything but novices at something like this. One of them called to his companions. All three of them halted and raised carbines to track the oncoming riders. Al Sutherland levelled his handgun and fired twice very fast, the result was not exactly what he had expected. His horse shied violently in mid-stride flinging the lawman through the air. He soared in spread-eagle fashion then dropped like a plummet. His riderless horse ran directly toward the stationary Mexicans.

Alvarado fired at the Mexican nearest him, shifted slightly and fired at the next man. The Mexicans had been concentrating on Sutherland because he had been closest to them. Alvarado had an advantage which lasted for about ten seconds, then the raiders faced half-around.

Alvarado held his body close from the waist up as he tried hard to aim. His mount had both ears pinned back trying to anticipate the next gunshot from above and behind his ears.

Alvarado fired. A Mexican in the act of squeezing off a carbine shot slammed back into his cantle and the carbine barrel was rising heavenward when he fired. Then the Mexican sagged, lost his Winchester, and fell.

Al Sutherland was able to aim for the first time as he lay flat out in the pale grass. He hit a Mexican who was firing at Bryan. The man hunched forward, head down. Sutherland fired his last round and the stunned man went down the rear side of his horse.

The remaining Mexican turned and spurred wildly after his companions down with the wagon. Constable Sutherland's horse followed this fleeing rider, head up, reins snapping and stirrups flopping.

Alvarado had difficulty getting his horse calmed. He made the animal walk back and forth as he approached the pair of downed raiders. By the time he had it quieted enough to be manageable Al Sutherland had come trudging up on foot, black in the face because now he was on foot and Lee Potter's wagon with its hoard and its outriders were beyond carbine range and still going.

Sutherland was breathing hard, his shirt was torn, his hands were scratched and as he stopped to pick up a Winchester he waited until Bryan swung down before saying, 'That gawddamned horse. He never shied like that before.'

Bryan gazed at the dishevelled large man. 'The way you landed I thought you'd had your wind knocked out.'

Sutherland had said all he had to say on this topic and approached the man he had shot twice, flipped him onto his back and gazed downward. 'Darned old fool. Bryan, he's sixty if he's a day.'

He was also dead.

The other raider, the one Bryan had shot, was also dead but had not died as quickly as his companion and had a beautiful rosary with carved ivory beads clutched in a mahogany-coloured hand.

Bryan pried it loose. The crucifix was solid gold filigree with raised characters in Latin. He held it out for the lawman to see but Sutherland was gazing in helpless frustration down where the wagon and its outriders were small in the distance.

Alvarado pocketed the rosary.

Something caught his attention near an arroyo on his left. It was a horse. It was picking grass as though it had already forgot that its rider's blood had fallen on its neck. The saddle was a Mex rig with an enormous horn, a slit down the middle of the tree and handmade, silver inlaid steel box stirrups. North of the border no one in his right mind rode steel stirrups. Down here a great many people did,

113

even ones who knew better.

Alvarado said, 'I have a feeling about that horse. It's not going to run.'

The constable squinted. 'Why don't those people breed some size into their horses?'

Without taking his eyes off the animal Bryan answered, 'You don't have to ride it, Al. You can lead it along like it was a dog. Hold my reins.'

The horse was not as small as he had seemed from a distance, but he was still no more than an eight hundred pound mount and Sutherland was a big-boned large man.

Bryan took his time walking his way up to the Mexican horse. The animal was gaunt from hard use and sweat-dark. His true colour was light bay but right now he looked seal-brown. He had been shod recently and the closer Bryan got to him the more it became apparent that this was a calm, quiet animal and despite having been abused did not appear to hate men.

Bryan was almost sorry when he reached for the dangling reins; what this animal needed was feed and care, not more riding. Al Sutherland called from the middle distance and pointed. There were riders breaking away from Valverde and except that they were all heading south there did not appear to be any order to the way they were moving, some were ahead, some were far back while others were spreading out easterly and westward.

114

Bryan walked back leading the Mexican horse, watching the horsemen as he approached Constable Sutherland. 'Its over,' he said.

He was correct, those were *bandeleros*, the raid on Valverde was finished. They were seen standing in the middle of empty range with two horses. At first it appeared the raiders might not be interested then two of them called to another pair and waved with their Winchesters. Those four turned away from their companions riding at a loose gallop.

Sutherland considered the Mexican horse, shook his head and said, 'We'd be better off doing this on foot anyway,' and knelt.

Bryan did the same. They were facing the four marauders with the sun behind them and in the faces of the Mexicans. Bryan pushed the Mexican carbine he had appropriated out and scowled at it. 'Most likely it wouldn't shoot straight for fifty feet. They're as bad as In'ians.' He raised the gun to slowly track a wildly flinging border-jumper. Evidently the Mexican saw sunlight reflecting off the barrel which was tracking him because he very abruptly reined hard around to the left, his animal dipping so low its rear toes flung soil and grit down the back of the rider's boots.

Sutherland shifted position and tracked another man. This time the Mexican fired his carbine with one hand, which was impressive to watch. The bullet went so far overhead it did

115

not scuff dust for three hundred yards—and Sutherland fired.

The raider yanked back so hard he pulled his horse half-around. It fell on its side, threshed frantically, sprang up and fled back toward Valverde. The Mexican did not move. His remaining companions halted and sat gazing from the prone raider to the distant kneeling figures of Alverado and Sutherland.

Bryan said, 'If they're In'ians they'll raise the yell and charge.'

Evidently they were not Indians. One of them fired a wild shot then turned to lope in the wake of the others. There was at least a mile separating them.

Sutherland stood up, shook off sweat and looked at the old saddlegun. 'True as true can be,' he said, looking incredulous.

There were people coming out of Valverde on horseback. It seemed to be the entire town. Alvarado walked over to the downed Mexican leading his horse. Sutherland remained back where they had been swearing like blue thunder because not only were the stirrups on his Mex outfit too short, but instead of being buckled they were laced with rawhide. To lengthen the stirrups would take at least an hour. He snugged up the cincha, looked his new horse in the eye and said, 'Now you behave yourself,' and vaulted into the saddle. The horse sagged briefly under more human weight than he had ever carried before, but stood like a rock. Sutherland squinted then leaned to stroke the animal's neck. 'Let's go,' he muttered. 'I just may keep you, *amigo*.'

Bryan looked up. Constable Sutherland riding his Mex outfit would have been a good New Mexican caricature of Sancho Panza and his burro, or whatever it was he rode.

Sutherland got down and frowned at the prone Mexican, 'I aimed for his brisket. That gun holds true.'

Bryan removed the Mexican's hat; there was a bloody gouge up one side of his head. The man was not dead, he was unconscious. Putting the hat back over the wound Bryan smiled. 'True as true can be,' he said. 'You aimed for the chest and creased him alongside the head. You better keep that gun Al. It might come in handy if you ever have to fight someone around a corner.'

Sutherland dropped to one knee. 'He ought to be dead even so. Are you sure he isn't?'

Bryan pulled down the filthy collar. There was a strong, even pulse beating in the raider's neck. Sutherland lifted the hat for a second look. It was a bloody wound and if the bullet had not struck on an angle to follow up around the curve of the Mexican's skull it would have gone inside and killed him.

Sutherland glanced up as the sound of riders reached him. Riders were everywhere, like angry ants after their hill had been kicked. He pushed the unconscious man's hat back over the wound and looked at his companion. 'Where were all these buffalo hunters when we needed them?'

Bryan did not change expression when he answered. 'It takes time to crawl out from under a bed and remove all the crates and whatnot from the door.' He too looked around. 'And besides a man could get hurt chasing after people.'

CHAPTER TWELVE

BLOOD IS RED

Valverde was a shambles. Two hours after the last raider had departed there was still dust in the air and the smell of burnt gunpowder.

The town was almost deserted. Now that the ire of its inhabitants had been aroused, their surprise and confusion dissipated by the two-hour fight in town, at least forty of its armed, angry inhabitants were in pursuit of the raiders. Slightly less than half of those pursuers were from Mex-town.

The injured town blacksmith told Sutherland and Alvarado this as they carried their injured raider into the jailhouse and locked him in a cell. The blacksmith had been hit in the upper left leg by a carbine bullet which had gone through without striking bone, making a clean wound which would heal properly. Even so the blacksmith would not be shoeing horses for a while.

There had been two people killed, both by gunfire, and nine injured including the blacksmith. Valverde's midwife had her cottage full and all her non-midwife skills were being taxed to their limits by the injured.

While the blacksmith was explaining all this in the jailhouse office Frank Miller, Juan Mendez, Jinglebob, Poker Flannery and big Jim Fisk walked in. They were still carrying Winchesters. They looked as disreputable as did all the other men in town.

The blacksmith hobbled away and Alvarado's rangeboss leaned back in a chair, fixed his employer with a stare and said, 'We saw you ride in with a live one.'

Sutherland was trying to make his stove work so they could have coffee and without looking around from doing this he said, 'There won't be any lynching, if that's what you got in mind. For one thing the prisoner's unconscious. For another he's all we got and I want some answers about this whole damned business.'

The Soledad man leaned solemnly to watch Al Sutherland working at the wood-stove. When he finally had a meagre flame flickering and closed the iron door, someone said, 'Naw; there's three more live ones.'

Sutherland turned. Bryan looked at his riders too. 'Alive?' he asked, and Juan Mendez nodded. 'Alive.'

'Where?'

'Over in the saloon. Chained over there,' stated Mendez.

The riders were regarding their employer solemnly. Sutherland stared at them in perplexity. 'Why didn't you fetch them over here an' lock them up?'

'Because,' replied big Jim Fisk, 'we couldn't find the key to the locks on their chains. I guess Potter took it with him.'

'Potter? You mean he chained these men?'

Fisk, shrugged. 'Seems so. They can only talk Mex. They talk it a mile a minute an' it's not like any Mex I ever heard before. Couldn't any of us make any sense out of what they were screamin' about.'

Juan Mendez faintly frowned. 'It's mostly some In'ian dialect. They're from the interior of Mexico, not the border territories.'

Juan then made a guess. 'I think that they either saw all that gold and tried to steal some, or maybe tried to steal it all. Anyway, Potter chained them with orders for them to be left behind when the others pulled out.'

There was a pause before Sutherland said, 'The bank?'

'Cleaned out,' stated Poker Flannery. 'Accordin' to some eyewitnesses when the raiders rode in from Mex-town they didn't make any attempt to sneak in; rode right down the roadway and when they was close one of 'em pitched a bomb or something against the bank window. The thing hit some steel grating and rolled back to the middle of the road. The raiders scattered real quick, and when the thing went off it blew that big hole in the roadway. Then the Messicans started shooting at everyone in sight from hidin' places. That's the first folks knew the town was being attacked. Half dozen people told me that same story.'

Al Sutherland clung to his question. 'The vault in the bank?'

Poker shrugged. 'Bryan, remember that strange noise we heard in the yard when old Velasquez rode in? That was the first bomb. Recollect when we was approachin' town there was a hell of a racket and it spooked our horses? Well, that was after Potter got his raiders all over behind the saloon on the east side of town, and that time they were able to put their bomb right in front of the safe's door . . . Accordin' to the clerk who worked at the bank, they got nine thousand dollars in gold an' silver.'

Sutherland scowled. 'The clerk wasn't hurt?'

'Yeah he was hurt, got a broken arm. He's around here somewhere. The Widow Billings splinted him.'

Sutherland looked at Bryan and wagged his head. 'What in hell would anyone with millions in gold and jewels want to risk his neck for another nine thousand dollars for?'

Bryan made a guess. 'To pay his border-jumpers. He most likely did not have that much cash himself, and they wouldn't take gold plunder; they'd already sold it to him. What they needed was cash money.'

Frank Miller went to stand in the open doorway. The dust was diminishing and the acrid scent of burnt gunpowder was too, but there were smashed doors, broken windows, glass lying everywhere and there were also bullet marks in almost all the building-fronts across from the jailhouse. Valverde looked like what it was; a town that had lived through a hard-fought battle.

He turned back when someone tapped his shoulder. Constable Sutherland was passing out coffee. Frank accepted a cup and eyed his boss. 'We should be after them, Bryan. Nine thousand dollars and all that other stuff. If they get over the line Scot-free a lot of folks on both sides of the border aren't goin' to sleep well for a long while.'

Juan Mendez spoke up. 'I don't think they will do that, Frank. There was a big soldier patrol down along the line. Tiburcio told me this morning that they sent three riders south to find the patrol and tell it what is happening up here. The soldiers will be riding north as Potter and his friends are riding south.'

Someone was sceptical. 'If they didn't send those riders out until this morning, Frank . . .'

'No. They sent them out yesterday, before the raiders hit Valverde.'

Al Sutherland was interested in this. 'How did they know day before yesterday there was goin' to be a raid?'

Juan Mendez spread his hands and smiled. 'The tortilla telegraph. That is the name Mexicans have for the rumours and information which flows both ways every day, from up here down there and from down there up here. Remember Constable, most of the people in Valverde have relatives in Old Mexico. They knew.'

Sutherland said he would pick a man or two on the way, and go after the chained men in the saloon. After he left Bryan asked if any of the men had been injured. None had. Jim Fisk held out his capacious shirt to show where a bullet had pierced it without touching him.

They went over to the cafe, the door of which had been shot half off its hinges. The proprietor was not around. He probably had been one of those enraged townsmen who had gone after Leland Potter and his *bandeleros*. Jinglebob who had been in a reticent mood since the fight had ended, stamped back to the cooking area and began to swear. 'it's a damned pig pen,' he

123

bawled. 'I never saw a kitchen this dirty in all my life!'

The tired men at the counter looked back and forth and one of them chuckled. 'Everything is back to normal,' he said, then they all laughed.

Jinglebob made a meal and sat upon the proprietor's side of the counter gorging with the others, and again he was reticent. The men knew his moods; this was the mood that it was better to ignore.

Someone mentioned casualties among the riders and that brought old Jinglebob's head up. Poker had seen three dead ones in the area around the saloon. Fisk had seen two more dead ones over in the general store. That seemed to end the discussion. Jinglebob put down his coffee cup and added one more.

'A little girl over in Mex-town. Her mother was shooing her into the house when some son-of-a-bitch in the alley out back of the saloon shot at them and hit the little girl in the head.'

Three dark, stained and sweaty horsemen reined up out front of the jailhouse, got tiredly down and walked over to the door. They paused to briefly turn and survey the ruined town. The men at the cafe saw their faces then. One was tall, gaunt, with a shock of iron-grey hair: Tiburcio Velasquez.

He had the ivory-handled sixgun in his hip-holster.

When the three Mexican horsemen entered

124

the jailhouse Alvarado's riders went back to their meal. Not very much was said until they had finished and were preparing to leave the cafe, then Jinglebob hung back after the others had passed out through the street-side opening with its broken doors. 'Juan,' he said, 'take a little walk with me.'

Mendez frowned. 'Where? What for?'

'I want to know if the woman saw the man who shot at them.'

Bryan led the others across to the jailhouse. Velasquez and his bronzed companions turned when they walked in. No one smiled nor offered a greeting. Velasquez and Constable Sutherland who had been talking, resumed their conversation. The Soledad men ranged along the walls of the little office listening.

There had been a fight about seven miles south of Valverde when the men from town caught Leland Potter and his *bandeleros* resting their animals in an overgrown arroyo which had water at the bottom.

Sutherland asked the question other men in the room had in mind. 'They let themselves get caught like that; no sentry watching?'

Velasquez replied matter-of-factly. 'Yes. They had a watcher. But I was in the lead with these riders from Mex-town. I told the others to wait. To stay far out and to watch the lower end of the arroyo so that if they came running out down there, they could catch them.' Tiburcio

125

shrugged and a faint look of annoyance crossed his face. 'It didn't happen that way . . . We four went into the underbrush on foot. The watcher was drinking water from a canteen sitting in shade.' Tiburcio rolled his eyes toward a stocky, impassive man. 'Jorge has done this before. He crawled on his belly. Something like that takes a long time.' Again Tiburcio shrugged. 'I guess the waiting men got impatient . . . Jorge finally was close enough to reach out with his bandanna and grab the watcher from behind and strangle him without a sound . . . We would have gone back and led the others up to the edge of the arroyo. It would have been like shooting fish in a rain barrel, but no, some of the townsmen went down a half-mile to close off the lower part of the arroyo and the others came charging up like Indians, yelling and firing before there was anything to aim at.' Tiburcio paused to meet Bryan Alvarado's gaze and quietly said something in Spanish, then resumed addressing Constable Sutherland.

'The *bandeleros* ran in all directions. Some of them even tried to ride their horses up our side of the arroyo which was too steep. We sat up there and shot them. Someone kept yelling in the underbrush down there but there was too much noise. The townsmen killed three raiders down where they had an ambush set up a half-mile down the arroyo.' Tiburcio smiled.

'That is all, *jefe*.'

Sutherland frowned. 'All? Wasn't Potter down there with his wagon?'

Velasquez nodded. 'Yes. One of the men from Mex-town is driving the wagon back with Leland Potter in it.'

'Dead?'

Tiburcio gazed pensively at the large lawman. 'Yes, dead. Of course dead. Everyone shot him a little. He was down there running around like a wild man, yelling for someone to help him, get the wagon out of there. We rode past and shot at him. All of us. The wagon should be here in an hour or so.'

Someone's pent-up long breath sounded loud as it was expelled near the back of the room.

Bryan spoke to the old man in Spanish. 'How many brigands escaped?'

No one knew. Tiburcio looked among his companions. They shrugged; they did not know and they did not care. Tiburcio spread his hands. 'I don't know. Not many, Maybe three or four. I don't know how many rode into Mex-town with Potter so I don't know how many men he attacked Valverde with. Maybe we will know in a few days. I know only that it did not seem to me that very many got away from the arroyo. It was only the ones who rode west. In the other three directions they did not have a chance.'

Al Sutherland shoved out a large hand.

Tiburcio shook it gravely without smiling. As he released the hand he said, 'You see . . . we lost three men killed and six wounded.' His dark eyes moved around the room. 'I wish you could have seen, *jefe*.'

Sutherland nodded sympathetically but the old man's eyes ignored that. 'I wish you could have seen them die protecting Valverde. I wish you could have seen something else, *jefe*; their blood is the same red colour as yours.'

For moments after Velasquez and his companions had departed there was an uncomfortable quiet, broken eventually by Al Sutherland. First he cleared his throat, then he faced the Soledad riders and said, 'Anyone here want to try and make sense out of what those fellers Lee Potter chained in the saloon have to say?'

No one answered. Sutherland said, 'Where's Mendez?'

Alvarado straightened up off the wall. 'I think we'd better go look for him, Al. Did you ask old Velasquez if he could understand your prisoners?'

'Yes. He wouldn't even go down into the cell room and look at them.'

At the door Bryan glanced back at the big lawman. 'You better watch for that wagon,' he said, and closed the door.

CHAPTER THIRTEEN

LEY FUGA

There was a kind of awkward, dazed system to the way people were beginning to clean up their town. They were mostly old men and women.

Far southward a cloud of dust showed riders coming toward town. People watched the dust with fear in their eyes but Constable Sutherland used his brass spy-glass to identify it as the men who had gone after Potter and his marauders.

Over in Mex-town it was very quiet, scarcely a person was abroad. The man named Garcia who operated a *cantina*, and who had a big thick nose, some gold in his mouth and coarse features, was sweeping hardpan soil in front of his business establishment and did not see the four sweaty, grave-faced men until the oldest among them spoke from behind in the dusty roadway. 'I put your horse back in his corral, washed his back and fed him.'

Garcia turned. The other three Mexicans were gazing at him too. He smiled broadly and leaned on the broom. 'You caught them then friends?'

The thickly-built Mexican wearing a red bandana spat aside before saying, 'Yes. Did you know our town lost some people killed and had others hurt?'

Garcia's face faded. 'I heard . . . Someone said the widow Garza's little girl was shot.'

'Dead,' stated another of the unsmiling men. 'Shot through the head . . . Garcia; where were you when we rode through calling for riders with arms to join us?'

The burly, very dark Mexican answered for Garcia. 'Hiding. He has a bad heart, didn't you know? He always has a bad heart when there is trouble.' Tiburcio turned to walk away and the last of his companions to follow along was the burly man, he called Garcia a contemptuous word and spat at his feet.

When they got to the edge of Mex-town Tiburcio stopped them in surprise. Someone had opened the faggot gate and his goats were wandering around eating everything green in sight. From inside the corral there was the sound of voices.

The burly Mexican stepped past old Tiburcio drawing his sixgun as he did so. He went almost up to the open gate then halted, listened for a moment, put up his gun and turned to beckon.

Juan Mendez and two other men were in the corral, which was fairly large. There was a third man; he looked terrible. His hat was gone, his clothing was torn and filthy and sweat was dripping from his face. He had a bluish welt across one cheek, it was too narrow to have been made by a fist; he had probably been

130

lashed across the face with a horseman's quirt.

One of the men with Juan Mendez heard something, aimed his sixgun toward the open gate and said, '*Quien es?*'

Tiburcio moved into sight, his companions in back. For a moment no one said a word then the man pointing the weapon holstered it and looked questioningly at Mendez.

Juan was squatting with his back to the faggot-fence behind him. He arose and said, 'This man has the name of Ponce Farias. He is from Sinaloa.'

Tiburcio and his companions entered the corral, walked over to stand with their backs to the faggots and stare at the Sinaloan. Ponce Farias had evil features, bloodshot eyes, and a bloodless slit of a mouth. Under different circumstances he would have been a man to fear. Now, with his jacket showing where crossed bandoleers had been, he was soaked with sweat and mute.

Juan Mendez spoke quietly. 'He was bucked off his horse when the other raiders were running from town and took refuge in a little house where a friend of mine found him . . . He attacked my friend with a knife and hurt him. These two men heard the noise and came to help. They took my friend over to the *gringa curandera* Billings. I brought this man to your corral, Tiburcio . . . We will help round up the goats when we are through.'

131

Tiburcio leaned on his corral gazing at the *bandelero*. 'Why didn't you just shoot him?' he asked.

A grizzled, weathered old man standing on the far side of Juan Mendez answered. 'Tiburcio; this man shot a little girl.'

Velasquez and the men with him gazed at the prisoner. One said, 'Friend, how do you know that?'

The grizzled man made a small death's-head smile. 'Because when we dragged him out of the shed into sunlight there was a woman being helped by two other women. She saw the man and began to scream and point. She fainted. The other women carried her to her house.'

Tiburcio looked at Juan Mendez. 'Yes?'

Mendez nodded. 'Yes. She saw him aiming at them, she knew his face.'

'And you brought him here?'

Juan Mendez looked directly into the eyes of the old man. '*Ley fuga, vierjo.*'

The burly man wearing a red bandanna with which he had strangled a marauder several hours earlier shook his head. 'He does not deserve it.'

Mendez neither agreed nor disagreed. He simply said, 'My friend that he stabbed in the shed works as the cook for Alvarado's ranch, Soledad. His name is Jinglebob. This one gave him no chance. But these men with me and I think we don't want to be like this Sinaloan.'

The burly man continued to gaze at the sweaty raider. He said no more, not until old Velasquez sighed, straightened up off the corral and turned toward the gate as he spoke to the burly man and the others who had accompanied him. 'The goats will eat everyone's gardens. Come, friends, and help me round them up.'

At the gate the burly man turned, spat, and told the prisoner when he met his friends in hell he should burn with them, then he disappeared beyond the enclosure and one of the men with Mendez lifted out his sixgun and spun the cylinder to be sure each hole contained a bullet. The sun was beating down; he squinted skyward, lowered his face and grinned. He was ready. The other man stood with thumbs hooked in his shellbelt also gazing at the prisoner. 'You did not answer,' he said in Spanish. 'When those others walked in you stopped talking. Answer now: Why did you shoot the little girl?'

Ponce Farias had reason to be afraid, and he was, but he was also a vicious, fierce man. His answer was curt. 'I thought in the dust she was a *gringa*.' His black eyes assayed his captors one at a time. 'If one kills the little ones they do not grow up to spawn more.'

Juan Mendez looked at the ground for a moment, then drew his sixgun and raised his face. 'Look behind you across the corral. That faggot fence is six feet tall so that coyotes cannot get in here and kill the old man's goats . . . I think the distance from here to there is what—seventy feet? If you jump high enough when you hit the faggots they will break and you may fall on the outside. If you do that you may live and go free.'

Ponce Farias shook sweat off his chin and raised a thick hand to wipe his lips and nose where more perspiration had been accumulating. He probably knew more about *ley fuga* than the men in front of him. He glared at them from narrowed eyes. 'If you kill me no one will know where there is a cache of gold church ornaments, some with diamonds and rubies and emeralds set in them.' The narrowed black eyes burned at the slouching men holding guns in their hands. 'It is worth more money than all of you together will earn in your lifetimes.'

Mendez nodded slightly. 'You wish to trade this for your life?'

'Yes.'

'Well; but maybe you are lying.'

Farias shook his head vehemently. 'It is the truth I swear it on the Cross.'

Juan pointed toward the ground with his gun barrel. 'Show us,' he ordered. 'Draw a map and show us.'

Farias's lips pulled down in scorn. 'I am not a child. You will shoot me after you know.'

Mendez raised his gun barrel and cocked the

weapon. 'We will shoot you if you don't draw the map.'

Ponce Farias looked around for a stick, a twig, something to draw in thick dust with. There was nothing so he shrugged and hunkered down, speaking as he began making a diagram. He told them of the landmarks, the nearest towns, he even named the ancient creekbed where the cache had been buried, and when he was finished and stood up his three captors gazed a long while at the map. Juan Mendez who did not know the country along the border where the cache was asked if his companions knew it. They did. They said they would take him down there tonight if he wished. Then one of them looked steadily at Ponce Farias. Speaking softly he said, 'Now you turn and run.'

Farias pulled straight up. 'I told you! I gave you this cache for my life! You agreed . . .'

The Mexican squeezed his trigger, the bullet struck between Farias's feet and he sprang aside, bent suddenly, swiftly, caught up a cupped handful of dust and goat droppings, flung it straight into the faces of his captors, and whirled to run.

He was not built for speed but this was the one time in his life when he had to force his body to do what it was not built to do, move very fast.

Mendez and his two companions did not raise

hands to their watering eyes, they blinked rapidly and waited, water making rivulets through dust on their faces.

Farias was almost to the far side of the corral, he gathered himself for the wild, hurtling leap. He struck the faggots near their spindly tops, and, as Juan Mendez had prophesied, they broke like match-sticks under his weight and momentum, showing dried splinters in all directions.

He was clawing to get over when the two men with Juan Mendez raised their sixguns at arm's length and fired. Farias became very briefly rigid and still. His arms and legs then threshed and Juan Mendez, aiming slightly higher than the back, fired one round.

Farias was knocked half-over the faggot fence, balanced there until the jerking started, then flopped back and fell in the dust.

The sound of people running broke through the silence which followed in the wake of the last gunshot-echo. Juan's companions did not look in the direction of the gate, they instead re-loaded. They thought it would be old Velasquez and his companions. It wasn't, it was Bryan Alvarado and three other men. They stopped in the gateway.

Bryan turned from the dead man toward his rider. 'Juan . . .?'

Mendez looked his employer straight in the eye. 'That is the man who killed a little girl. He was trying to get away.'

Bryan looked straight back for a moment, then looked at the men loading their weapons, considered the distance across the corral and looked back. He lifted his hat, mopped off sweat and re-settled the hat. 'Where is Jinglebob?'

'That *bandelero* stabbed him. He is over at Widow Billings's place.'

Big Jim Fisk frowned. 'Bad off, Juan?'

'He lost a lot of blood, Jim. These two men carried him over there.'

Frank Miller was showing a poker face. 'We better go see,' he said to Bryan. 'Maybe there's something we can do for him. Sure as hell there's nothing we can do here.'

Bryan looked again at the corpse, then at his rider. 'We'll meet at the jailhouse in a little while,' he said and led the men away.

One of Juan Mendez's companions looked thoughtfully toward the empty gate. 'They knew, I think,' he said in Spanish.

Juan nodded. 'They knew.'

Old Tiburcio and his companions came as far as the gate opening and solemnly looked in. Velasquez made a little gesture. 'I can't get the goats to go in there as long as they can smell blood.'

Everyone went with the old man over to his little mud house, picked up tools and marched back to drag the body out and cover the blood with dirt. The day was well along. It was still hot but less so than it had been earlier. When the goat corral met with Tiburcio's approval he pointed to the body and said, 'That *pelado*—that nobody—what will you do with him?'

The men leaned on their tools dispassionately eyeing the dead man. One of them said, 'I will get my horse and drag him out a mile or two and leave him.'

Tiburcio looked at the speaker with smouldering eyes. 'Do you know,' he said in archaic Spanish, 'that if you do that his spirit will enter your *cojones* and all of your children will be born dead?'

At once the speaker offered a fresh suggestion. 'We can all take him out and dig a deep grave.'

Tiburcio shook his head. 'No. Tonight after dark we will bury him in the mission churchyard among all the other graves.'

'Him!' exclaimed the burly Mexican. 'Him; this killer of small children! This raider of towns! This rider of other people's horses!'

Tiburcio drew himself up. He was tall for a Mexican and forty years earlier had been even taller. He glowered at them. 'Look at him. What do you see? His back is to us. Now, friends, black as his soul is, he knows something we do not know. He leaves behind the worst of him and we should bury it decently because we are *gentes de razon* . . . Tonight after dark. Now I will cover him with some canvas and you can help me get the goats into the pen.'

Juan Mendez left them walking slowly back up through Mex-town. There still was very little activity around him, but when he emerged from the dog-trot into *gringo*-town, everything seemed different. There was a head-hung team of horses drowsing in harness to a battered old wagon over in front of the jailhouse, Northward, Bryan and the other Soledad riders were standing on the porch of the Widow Billings's place. Juan started toward them.

CHAPTER FOURTEEN

A WOMAN

Fisk, Flannery, Miller and Alvarado were solemn. Juan came through the gate looking up at them on the porch and was sure he read death in their faces, and faintly frowned as he reached the steps. 'It wasn't that bad a wound,' he told them.

Bryan answered. 'Bad enough. Jinglebob's old.'

'Then he's dead?'

'No. But it will be a long time before he's able to do much.' Bryan considered Juan

139

Mendez. 'What did your prisoner say about shooting the little girl?'

'That he thought it was a little *gringa*.'

'And that made it all right?'

Mendez's gaze hardened. 'It wouldn't have made it all right no matter who the little girl belonged to . . . Did the constable put the money and Potter's loot back?'

None of them had an answer to that so they all turned southward down through the town where people were sweeping up broken glass, bringing dirt to fill the hole in the road, and some were even puttying bullet holes in their walls. The smell of dust and gunpowder was gone. Valverde was already beginning to heal, and the dead had not even been buried yet.

Sutherland's office was full of townspeople who were mostly all speaking at once and trying to out-shout one another. When the Soledad men walked in most of the complaining dwindled. Constable Sutherland, looking embattled behind his desk, arose and beckoned through the crowd toward his back room. He stood beside the doorway as the Soledad men pressed forward.

Leland Potter was on his back. Someone, perhaps the constable, had tossed an old brown army blanket over most of him, which was just as well.

There were several other bodies in the back room, lined out side by side and fully covered with the same colour blankets, which had come from the bunks in the cells.

Bryan turned back. The milling townspeople became silent as he went toward the desk and waited for Sutherland to close the door and meet him over there. Then he explained about Jinglebob, and the man named Farias who had killed a little girl over in Mex-town and had been shot while trying to escape.

Al Sutherland gazed a moment at Alvarado, then looked past as he said, 'Clear out. All of you. It's over. When I get time I'll call a meeting at the fire-house and tell you all I know. Now clear out!'

When the little office was empty Sutherland sat down and pointed to benches and chairs as he said, 'I don't know how much stuff was in Lee's cache but I got one hell of a lot of it locked in my storeroom an' until I know what's to be done with it I'll post armed guards.' Sutherland looked around at the tired, whiskery faces. 'All the money from the bank wasn't there. About half of it isn't. There was some in the saddlebags and pockets of the dead raiders. My guess is that when we get through lookin' for it and can make a tally we'll maybe have about three-quarters of it. I guess those border-jumpers who got away took the rest of it with them.' Sutherland leaned on his desk. 'Maybe the army will recover it. Old Velasquez told me they sent some riders from Mex-town down to the border to hunt up a patrol a few days back . . . Will Jinglebob make it?'

Bryan nodded. 'Yes. But it'll be a while before he'll dance a fandango.'

Al Sutherland glanced in the direction of his cell-room door. 'I got more prisoners than this jailhouse was built for,' he said and arose to cross to a little barred front-wall window.

Frank Miller asked about the man the rest of them had forgotten. 'What about Charley Bright, the horsethief we brought in before this other mess busted loose?'

The constable turned. 'He's comin' right along. I'd say he'll be able to walk to the gallows if the time comes for that.'

Frank sat looking thoughtfully at the floor for a moment then said, 'How do we find out which one shot old Jake Monroe?'

No one knew although Constable Sutherland thought that by the time he was through questioning his prisoners it was possible he could have an answer.

He looked at the rumpled, drawn, tired men and said, 'Valverde owes you.'

Bryan stood up. 'I guess we'd better get back to the yard,' he said, and nodded at the lawman as he led his riders out of the jailhouse. Poker and Jim Fisk looked over at the saloon with its locked front doors and sighed, then followed the others down to the opposite end of town for their horses.

142

The liveryman and a squatty, pock-marked Mexican hostler who looked totally villainous until he smiled, then he resembled a smoked cherub, greeted the Soledad men as though they were long lost brothers. They were so full of talk that Alvarado and his men did not have to say much as they rigged out, and later, leaving town on a northwesterly course when the men looked back, Juan Mendez said, 'I told Tiburcio Velasquez to keep that gun with the ivory handles. Maybe that was wrong. Maybe the constable will want it.'

Alvarado did not think so. 'He's got what he wanted; Leland Potter and the gold.'

When they entered the yard and instinctively looked in the direction of the cookhouse Poker sighed then reined to the barn tie-rack and spoke as he was dismounting. 'Can you cook, Juan?'

Mendez stopped moving and stared. Poker saw the look and sighed again. 'I guess not. How about you, Jim?'

'I'm the only person west of the Missouri River who burns water tryin' to boil it.'

'Frank . . .?'

The rangeboss shook his head as he hauled off the saddle, shouldered it and started into the barn. Poker lifted down his saddle and blanket to follow Frank Miller. 'There's goin' to be some skinny scarecrows around here by the time Jinglebob gets back,' he muttered.

It was not quite that bad. None of them were cooks, but every one of them had done some cooking. Even Bryan came down early in the following mornings because he could cook eggs and make coffee. But not everyone appreciated his eggs; he put hot sauce in them, sliced cloves of garlic to sprinkle over them, and after the third day when the cookhouse was beginning to smell like a Mexican barracks big Jim Fisk arose from the breakfast table with a smile for his employer and said Bryan had been cooking long enough, now Jim would take over, and out in the yard when Bryan and Juan Mendez met Juan furrowed his brow. 'Not even Apaches eat food that hot,' he said. Bryan nodded. 'I know,' he replied and went over to disappear inside the barn leaving Juan gazing after him. Suddenly Mendez laughed.

It was on the fourth day after the raid on Valverde and the Soledad crew was returning in mid-afternoon from the calving grounds that Constable Sutherland arrived in a top-buggy. They had never seen him drive out before, he had always come out a-horseback.

He was waiting at the tie-rack in front of the barn when the crew arrived. There was a woman sitting in the rig. She had raven's-wing black hair that came to a marked widow's peak in the centre of a broad, unmarred forehead. She had very dark eyes and a faintly golden-tan complexion. Each rider tried not to stare as they

144

swung off. Al Sutherland smiled at Bryan Alvarado and nodded toward the woman in the buggy. 'This is *Señora* Obregon. *Señora*, this is Bryan Alvarado.'

The beautiful woman did not smile nor speak but she barely inclined her head. Bryan covered his perplexity by asking if the *Señora* and Al Sutherland would care to come over to the main-house out of the sunlight.

He led the way. When they reached the porch he shoved open the door and stepped back. As the startlingly beautiful woman moved past she spoke in almost accentless English. 'This is kind of you.' Then she was inside. Sutherland moved up, threw Bryan a look and rolled his eyes, then followed the beautiful woman.

The parlour was cool and gloomy. Bryan draped his hat from a wall-peg, offered *Señora* Obregon a chair and offered wine but neither she nor Constable Sutherland responded favourably as Bryan sat down wondering what else he should do. The woman solved that for him by saying, 'Mister Alvarado. I came with the government officials from Mexico to inspect the boxes in Constable Sutherland's office.'

Bryan shot a look at Sutherland, who almost imperceptibly nodded his head.

The woman's very dark eyes were fixed on Bryan's face. 'Mister Sutherland and others told us the part you and your riders had in fighting

145

the *pronunciados* and recovering the treasure.'

Bryan frowned a little. '*Pronunciados*? I thought they were border-jumpers as we call them up here; run-of-the-mill marauders.'

The beautiful woman paused a moment before saying, 'In Mexico it is not often an easy distinction, Mister Alvarado. They were marauders; outlaws. In Mexico we call them pirates.' The dark eyes showed a very faint glow of sardonic humour. 'It is Mexican law, Mister Alvarado, that pirates are to be put to death when they are captured.'

Bryan nodded. 'Yes,' he said dryly, 'I know.'

If the woman detected disapproval she did not show it when she continued to speak. 'What they were doing, Mister Alvarado, was looting the border provinces and selling what they stole to someone for American money. That money they were also using to buy arms—even American cannons and Gatling guns. They were storing these things against the day they would have enough to raise and put an army of revolutionaries into the field against the national government.'

Bryan shot Al Sutherland another look and, as before, Sutherland nodded his head very slightly to verify what the beautiful woman was saying.

Bryan must have looked incredulous to the beautiful woman because she finally smiled at him. He had no idea what her age was, but

146

when she smiled it made her look no more than perhaps sixteen or seventeen. But since she was a *Señora* rather than a *Señorita*, she was a married woman. That made Bryan believe she was older than she looked.

'You thought it was simply a raid, Mister Alvarado?'

He nodded at her. He'd had no reason to think it was anything else. He'd heard of no revolt in Mexico, not lately anyway. But of course he wouldn't have heard of a revolt in this instance because there had not been one—it was in the offing, it had not actually happened yet.

The beautiful woman glanced around the large old parlour with its portraits of Bryan's parents and grandparents, all unsmiling in the *gachupín* tradition. She too seemed to be a little puzzled. Eventually she said, 'I was asked to come out to your ranch and tell you that my government is grateful for what you have done. You and Mister Sutherland, your *vaqueros*, all the people who broke the back of the *pronunciados* . . . including the other Americans, the ones who live over in—Mex-town.'

When she said it, it sounded degrading. Bryan shifted in the chair. He and everyone else had always referred to it as Mex-town. Even its own residents referred to it that way. The beautiful woman made it sound like an accusation. He thought she may never had heard the term, 'gourd-town' for the poorer, more squalid Mexican villages down closer to the border. It was probably as well that she hadn't.

She arose and held out her closed fist toward Bryan. He stood up too and when she told him to hold his palm out he obeyed. She dropped a golden rosary with carved ivory beads into his hand and smiled up at him as she did it. 'In appreciation, Mister Alvarado.'

He gazed at the rosary. 'I can't take this,' he said, raising his eyes to her.

She spoke softly. 'This is not from my government. It is from me, Mister Alvarado ... That man you proved to be the *norteamericano* buyer of looted gold. The man who was getting very rich from helping to arm *pronunciados* to kill and murder in Mexico—Leland Potter—he and two of the *pronunciados'* leaders ambushed and killed two Mexican army officers who were sent to the border provinces when it was learned in Mexico City there were men preparing a revolution ... One of those officers was my husband, Mister Alvarado. That happened three years ago ... Will you please keep the rosary, from me?'

He closed his fingers over the rosary and smiled. 'Thank you, *Señora*. I wish I could have done more.'

Al Sutherland, standing slightly to one side, hat in hand watching, got an odd expression on

148

his face and did not lose it until Bryan went to hold the door for the beautiful woman to leave the house. Then Sutherland marched out too, and avoided looking at Bryan.

The sun was a circular red stain upon the darkening westerly horizon and down across the yard someone had fired up the cook-stove in the cookhouse.

Bryan smelled meat frying and offered his guests dinner, then remembered it might not be very good and was beginning to warn them when Al Sutherland said, 'By the way, Jinglebob told Widow Billings that if you don't come get him by tomorrow afternoon he's going to start walking home.'

Bryan explained to the beautiful woman who Jinglebob was. She said, 'I was educated in New York . . . Why would someone be called Jinglebob? I never heard that before.'

Bryan felt Sutherland grinning and did not look at him. '*Señora*, a jinglebob is one of those little steel tassels some men have on their spurs near the rowel.' He looked to see if she understood. She did not seem to. He then said, 'Well, not many men have them on their spurs any more but when Jinglebob was first hired at Soledad ranch, he was wearing spurs with those little things on them, and ever since I can remember that's what he's been called.'

They reached the top-buggy and Al Sutherland went over to untie the dozing horse

149

between the shafts. He seemed to be taking an awfully long time doing it.

The beautiful woman looked up at Bryan. 'He has another name?'

Bryan nodded. 'Yes . . . I don't remember what it is.'

She looked surprised, then she laughed. Sutherland was still untying the horse. Bryan shot him a look but the constable's head was down, he was not watching them. Bryan took down a shallow breath and opened the hand with the rosary in it. 'Will you be in Valverde very long, *Señora*?' he asked, looking at the rosary, not the beautiful woman.

'I don't know. Arrangements are being made for some of your soldiers to accompany our coaches as far as the border with the treasure. Down there, we are to be met by Mexican lancers to accompany us the balance of the way. It takes time for all the arrangements to be made.'

Bryan was perspiring. 'The hotel in Valverde had most of its windows shot out,' he said. 'There will be funerals.' He finally looked at her. 'I offer you my hospitality for as long as you stay.'

The very dark eyes became still. 'It is kind of you, but I should stay in Valverde. There are six of us on this mission for our government. It would be better if we were together.'

Bryan nodded.

The beautiful woman suddenly said, 'But Sunday no one works in Valverde, do they?'

Bryan shook his head and finally Al Sutherland got the horse untied and moved beside it to tie the shank to a loop in the collar. Then he looked over the horse's back at them. They did not seem aware of him until he said, 'Ma'am, you can have this buggy Sunday if you'd like.'

Señora Obregon turned away from Bryan and smiled at Sutherland. 'That's very kind of you,' she said, and stepped up under the buggy-top, seated herself and looked steadily at Bryan Alvarado as the constable came around and grunted up to the seat at her side.

Bryan moved closer. 'In the morning, *Señora?* We ride over the ranch if you'd like . . . There is a little lake. We could have a picnic up there under the trees.'

The black eyes brightened. 'In the morning, Mister Alvarado. Next Sunday.'

Sutherland talked up the buggy mare and made a big swing out of the yard, as they were lining out in the direction of Valverde he leaned out and looked back where Bryan was standing like a stone statue.

The woman said, 'Constable,' and Sutherland straightened up on the seat. 'Yes'm.'

'Did Mister Alvarado's wife die?'

Al blinked. 'No ma'am. As far as I know he's never been married.'

She turned wide dark eyes. 'But why?'

Sutherland had no answer to offer. He drove a short distance then said, 'Well, I don't exactly know except that some men just don't seem to get married.'

She sat in thought for a while before speaking again. 'He doesn't look Mexican.'

'He isn't, ma'am. His mother was Irish, they tell me. His father comes from a line of native New Mexicans.'

She said '*Gachupínes?*'

Sutherland tried to remember if he'd heard the term before, and decided that if he had, he did not now know what it meant so he asked her to define the term. She said. 'It's not really a good word; it only means people who wear spurs. In my country a long time ago the only people allowed to ride horses and wear spurs were the Spanish, or the *criollos*—people of Spanish descent who were born in Mexico instead of Spain.'

Sutherland was a native of Texas, he was therefore not unaware that Mexicans had some pretty complicated social distinctions, but this was one he had not heard of before. He thought about it and finally said, 'I guess you could say Bryan's father's folks were—what did you call them?'

'*Gachupínes.*'

'Yeah. Like that, I guess.'

It was evening by the time they got back to

Valverde where Al Sutherland let the handsome woman off in front of the hotel then took the rig down to the liverybarn to leave it. On his walk back to the jailhouse he shook his head. The Mexican officials had been in town two days; almost three days and although he'd had contact with every one of them in that length of time this was the first time he'd seen the beautiful woman act as though she were not made of iron.

At the office he had to light a lamp and the moment he did that noises began down in his cell-room, so he kicked the door closed, fired up the stove because he expected to have to remain at the jailhouse until late, which he'd had to do every night since the raid, then went over to the cafe which was now being operated by a seasoned campaigner; the same grumpy cafeman except that now after having taken part in the pursuit and fight with the border-jumpers his entire personality had changed. He met the constable's gaze with a wise expression and said, 'You'll be wantin' pails of grub for the prisoners, eh?' and when Sutherland nodded the cafeman pointed. 'Set down. I'll get you a cup of coffee. It'll take me a few minutes.'

Sutherland sat down, turned sideways and gazed out the freshly-glazed new glass in the window frame. There were lights nearly the full length of his town, which was unusual except that these were unusual days.

The cafeman returned burdened with food

pails which he lined up on the counter and surprised Al Sutherland by making an expansive gesture as he said, 'No charge, Constable. Us folks who uphold the law got to help one another out. Just bring back the pails.'

Al got across the road and inside his office. He was putting the pails on a table when Jinglebob opened the door and stepped in. Jinglebob had been shaved, his clothes were clean, his hat had even been brushed, but he was pale. His lips were fixed in a stubborn way as he eyed the big lawman. 'Well, they comin' for me or do I start walking?'

Bryan had not said whether he would come to town for his cook or not. Sutherland pointed toward a bench and said, 'Sit down. I got to feed the prisoners.' He took the pails down into the cell-room and shoved them beneath the doors. His prisoners were hungry men, even the one with the big bandage on his head. Several tried to strike up a conversation but Sutherland turned on his heel, returned to the office, slammed and barred the thick oaken door and gazed at Jinglebob. 'Tomorrow's Saturday,' he said.

The old man eyed him. 'Yeah, usually is when today is Friday. They comin' or not?'

'How about if you was to lie over until Sunday,' said Sutherland, heading for his chair at the desk.

Jinglebob drew himself up. 'I'm not goin' to

154

lie over until Sunday. I'm goin' to start walkin' first thing in the morning.'

'You can't do it, Jinglebob. You got stabbed and . . .'

'I can too, Constable, and I'm goin' to do it!'

Sutherland leaned on the desk eyeing the angry older man. 'Jinglebob, there's a beautiful woman going to drive out to the ranch Sunday morning. You could ride with her.'

The old man's eyes narrowed. 'What beautiful woman?'

'Her name is Obregon, she came up here about that stolen Mex gold and whatnot.'

'Why is she goin' out to the yard? We didn't steal anything.'

Al Sutherland hunched forward and dropped his voice a little more than a whisper. 'She was out there today. Sunday she's goin' back out there then her and your boss are goin' riding . . . have a picnic somewhere on the range.'

Jinglebob's brow cleared, his eyes grew fixed on the lawman's face. 'When the hell did this happen, Constable?'

'Today. Now remember, this is just between the two of us. Nobody else knows. Now then, do you want to wait until Sunday morning and ride out with her?'

Jinglebob stroked his jaw and scowled. 'Real pretty is she?'

'Prettiest woman you ever saw.'

'Well . . . does she know I'll be riding

155

along?'

'No. I'm goin' up to the hotel right now to tell her.'

'Maybe she won't want me along, Constable.'

Sutherland raised his brows and leaned back. 'Won't want . . . Jinglebob she thinks you're a genuine hero. All you fellers from Soledad ranch.'

Jinglebob relaxed against the wall. 'Well, come right down to it we did do a pretty good job . . . All right, I'll ride out with her Sunday morning . . . Real pretty?'

Sutherland rolled his eyes. 'Wait. Just wait until you see her. You never in your life saw a woman as pretty. Never.'

Jinglebob arose, flinched slightly, then headed for the door. 'I'd better get a bottle of French toilet water,' he muttered. 'And shave Saturday night.'

After the door closed Constable Sutherland lowered his head, putting his face into his hands and heaved a big sigh. When his month was over with he'd be as happy as a kitten in a box of shavings. As for Bryan Alvarado, if he let that beautiful woman get away he deserved whatever evil fate might befall him. And if some son-of-a-bitch would open the saloon for business again Sutherland would be a grateful customer.